"It's escapism," he said.
"An adolescent fantasy!"

"But I long to see him again," Merril said.

"Then why don't you?"

"I have a job. I can't just pack up and go when I feel like it," she snapped.

"I'd like to shake some sense into you!" Torrin said angrily. "But I've got a better idea."

Torrin gripped her arm and propelled her to the door. Outside was a large sleek black Jaguar with smoked-glass windows.

"Where are we going?" Merril protested, even as the door closed behind her and Torrin settled in the driver's seat.

The car swept powerfully down the road before he answered. "If you haven't yet realized it, Miss Merril Park, you're being kidnapped."

SALLY HEYWOOD

fantasy lover

Harlequin Books

TORONTO • NEW YORK • LONDON
AMSTERDAM • PARIS • SYDNEY • HAMBURG
STOCKHOLM • ATHENS • TOKYO • MILAN

Harlequin Presents first edition September 1989
ISBN 0-373-11200-9

Original hardcover edition published in 1988
by Mills & Boon Limited

CHAPTER ONE

A STRONG brown hand shot out, dragging Merril into
the safety of a doorway. From further up the street
came the rattle of machine-gun fire and she found
herself jerked back hard into her rescuer's arms as
she tried to peer out to see what was going on. She
could feel the stranger's tall, muscular body pressing
against her own, and for a moment she was vibrantly
conscious of the long length of it, his arms gripping
her tightly in a sort of embrace before she managed to
struggle free.

'Stay inside. You'll get your head blown off!' he
rasped.

Her eyes swivelled back at him in astonishment.
'You speak English!'

With a white cloth wrapped native-style over his
head, obscuring most of his face, she could only see
his eyes and a slash of sunburned skin above the
dazzling cloth but a change in the honey brown of
their expression hinted at a smile, despite the danger
of the situation. The man gave a throaty chuckle full
of mischievous amusement. 'Don't look so
surprised!' He didn't go on to explain but gestured to
keep quiet. Some soldiers, rebels, Merril guessed,
clattered past the narrow doorway. As if he feared
she might make some giveaway movement, putting
them both in danger again, he dragged her roughly
into his arms, placing one warning hand over her
mouth.

For a moment all danger was forgotten and Merril
became aware only of being locked intimately in his

arms. Her limbs softened against him despite her fear, and they clung together for what seemed like an age as the sounds outside advanced and receded. She could hear the in and out of his breathing, smell the scent of a kind of sun-oil he wore and feel the roughness of his Army shirt against her burning cheek. The moment might have gone on for ever if he hadn't bent his head and whispered in his hoarse voice, 'You're one of the foreign correspondents?'

She nodded, too scared to speak now that the noise of fighting outside was increasing again.

'You're the first one to show a face outside the hotel bar,' he grinned, then shushed her reply as voices were heard just outside their hiding place.

Merril and Rory, her photographer, and somebody from a French daily had left the hotel at ten o'clock that morning, as soon as they heard a rumour that there was going to be some action. They had been inside the hotel ever since they arrived twenty-four hours ago, and the news desk was already on to Merril, demanding a story to justify her air fare. It had been bad luck to get caught in the crossfire like this, but as soon as everything was quiet again she would make her way back to the hotel. With any luck Rory would have some decent pictures to show for their adventure. She whispered all this as they clung together in the shadow of the doorway.

A strong smell of carbide was drifting in from the street, but the sounds of fighting were more distant now. More disturbing was the effect of being locked in the arms of this exotic stranger.

Merril felt her senses swoon, then she shook herself. This was no time for thoughts like that! She was a professional journalist, just as her father had been, and she was here to do a job, not to wilt over some dashing stranger!

Mercifully his grip had slackened as soon as he was

sure the soldiers had gone on down the street, and he was looking at her now with a quizzical expression in his eyes, one arm still round her shoulders. Despite the danger of imminent discovery he seemed totally unafraid, and a devilish expression came into those compelling brown eyes as he let his glance run appreciatively over her figure in its jeans and clingy T-shirt.

She wriggled from his touch, blazingly aware of the war-honed muscles beneath the white scarf draped over what looked like combat trousers and regulation Army shirt.

'Don't go outside!' He let her step away from the protection of his arms without trying to stop her, but his gravelly voice held a warning note that brought an involuntary shiver. Merriel turned back.

'They won't shoot me. They'll see I'm a foreign journalist,' she protested, annoyed at being told what to do.

'Do you think they'll be impressed by that?' he demanded drily in the same hoarse whisper. 'These people are trained to shoot first and question afterwards.'

Despite his words his gaze lingered over the bright mop of blonde hair and he looked as if he was going to say something else, but just then another burst of firing broke out, there were yells and a stampeding of heavy feet, and the man grasped her by the shoulder and hurried her further back into the building.

It had once been somebody's home, but now it was gutted by war, its walls pocked by bullets, a hole gaping in one corner where something large had driven into it.

'We can't stay here. Follow me.' He strode over to a door in the wall at the back of the house, peering round it with trained caution, beckoning to her to hurry after him. Merril found herself in a small alley, and before she could call out he had started to run alongside it, half crouching, looking back now and then to make sure she was following. When he reached an intersection in the honeycomb of little passages, he waited for her to catch up.

'See that building over there?' he rasped, pointing to a gutted office block further up the hill. She followed the direction of his glance and saw a four-storey building, its windows smashed, debris strewn across the piazza in front of it. 'When I tell you to go, I want you to run like hell and don't stop till you get inside. OK? Once there you should be safe for the time being. Ready?'

'Wait! Why should I——?'

'Ready?' he repeated, one hand gripping her shoulder.

'No—listen! Where are you going——?'

'Do you always stand and argue like this? Do as you're told, damn you!' His demeanour was suddenly so savage, she felt she had no alternative but to do as he ordered. As soon as she heard his command, she ducked her head and ran as fast as she could over the open ground between their shelter and the office block. Before she had gone half-way she knew why he had told her to run. The pattering sound of bullets broke out almost at once, and she tried to zigzag just as she had seen in countless films. But instead of little spurts of dry dust being kicked up around her feet as she expected there was nothing but unbroken, hard-packed earth, and she realised that the gunmen were aiming in another direction altogether.

When she reached the sanctuary of the gutted building, she turned her head and saw that her companion was running along the top of a low wall. He must be mad! she thought. He's clearly visible, an easy target. Then she understood what he was doing. In a moment he had jumped down on to the piazza, and making full use of available cover like a professional gained the safety of the building a few seconds later.

'You fool!' she burst out. 'You deliberately drew their fire! You must be mad!'

He adjusted the protective cloth across the lower part of his face again and for a second she saw the brief dazzle of even white teeth.

'Not mad, chivalrous! After all, you are a lady!' He gave that deep-throated chuckle again. 'Are you all right?'

'Of course I am,' Merril snapped, resenting the fact that he seemed to think she needed wrapping in cotton wool. 'But what do you think you're doing, dragging me right up here? It's going to be even more difficult to work our way back to the other side now. Don't you realise we're right behind rebel lines?' Everything was quiet outside and she made for the door. 'I'm going back down. I've got a story to file—I can't hang about up here. I don't know why the hell I followed you!'

He grabbed her roughly by the forearm as she moved away, and held her in a grip that hurt. 'Look here, you're not going anywhere yet. It's a complete shambles down there. Nobody knows who the hell they're taking pot shots at, and I'm not having you finishing up dead . . . Keep still!' he commanded as she started to struggle. 'They'll be busy out there for quite some time. You'll have to sit it out.'

'Don't you tell me what I have to do! Who do you think you are? And let go—you're hurting!' His grip was amazingly strong and Merril guessed that under the concealment of his battle-gear he would have muscles like bands of steel.

She glanced down at her trembling hands, and the

strong brown one wrapped tightly round her wrists, then glanced up at him with an elfish smile. 'All right—I guess you win. Now take your hands off, please. I promise to behave.'

'Good girl!'

Merril greeted this sort of remark as she always did, with a scowl. 'I'm twenty-three,' she informed him coldly, 'hardly a girl, thank you.'

'You look about sixteen. What on earth have they sent you out here for?'

'Oh, yes, you would ask that,' she tossed her head, 'that's a typical male reaction!'

'Not at all. It's simply unusual to find someone like you in a place like this. You have to admit,' he grinned disarmingly, 'you're not the usual whisky-sodden, chain-smoking reporter. You must work for an unusually enlightened editor.'

'There was only a rumour of trouble before I left England. If they'd imagined it was going to turn out to be anything risky, they'd have sent one of the men for sure,' she admitted candidly. 'They always get the exciting assignments.'

'This is exciting enough for you, isn't it?'

'It would be if I could get down there to see what was going on,' she grumbled, half turning to the door again.

'Look, sweetheart, you wouldn't see much even if you did go down,' the man rasped in his strangely sexy voice. 'One gun pointing at your head looks much like another. And believe me, nobody knows who they're shooting at right now. It's total panic and confusion.'

'But I've got to get a story! If my news editor thinks I copped out, he'll never send me anywhere like this again!'

'He won't be able to send you anywhere if you're dead. Be sensible.' Then he smiled again, softening the effect of his warning. 'What are you worried about? That it'll be the Chelsea Flower Show and man bites dog for evermore?' He was still holding her by the arm, though his grip had relaxed, and his sharp eyes sparked over her, restless and alert.

'Who are you?' Merril demanded. 'You're not a journalist yourself, are you?'

'Definitely not.'

'Then you must be part of some security force the goverment hasn't told us about——'

'Wrong again, and even if I were, a journalist would be the last person I'd tell!'

'Fair enough,' she agreed as if she wasn't really interested. But she looked thoughtful. 'Been out here long, then?' She opened her lustrous blue eyes in a look of calculated innocence that never failed to elicit the information she wanted. This time as a ploy, however, it was a disastrous failure.

'Don't ask questions——'

'And you'll tell me no lies,' she finished for him, turning away. She *would* find out who he was, because as far as she knew this was a local conflict. News of any official involvement would be a scoop to end scoops. If she was the only one on to it she would hit the headlines in a big way, and that would make the news editor sit up!

Conscious that her companion was still holding her by the arm, she made herself draw closer, passing a hand over her brow as she wilted against him. 'It's so hot! Nobody warned me it was going to be like this.'

Unmoved by the seductiveness of her body pressing against his, he disengaged the hand which had somehow found its way on to his forearm and pushed her towards a jumble of furniture beside what had once been an elevator. 'Better take the weight off your feet if you're feeling faint,' he suggested humorously. 'We're in for a long wait.'

He went over to lean against the doorpost, folding his arms across his expanse of chest and dropping his head as if instantly asleep.

Once she'd got over her pique at being so abruptly dismissed, Merril had to admit he looked sort of picturesque standing there in the doorway in his battle-gear. He was tall, about six foot two or so, marvellously broad-shouldered and, with his face hidden, had an aura of toe-tingling mystery.

I must find out what he's doing here, she told herself. His current indifference suggested he didn't much like blondes, but she'd get friendly enough to get his story. She'd have to. Her perennial bugbear, Ray Doyle, the news editor, would expect it. And, even without Ray breathing down her neck, she was desperate to prove herself. Apart from that, to be honest, she wanted to discover every last thing she could—who this man was, what he was doing here, where he belonged . . . and with whom.

Minutes passed. She should have been bored, champing at the bit, but, despite the rumble of distant gunfire and the knowledge that she was probably missing the best story of her life, it was strangely pleasant sitting here. The sun spilled in strong bright bars across the coloured tiles of the floor, and her companion, desperately romantic-looking in his white burnous thing, was making her imagination run riot. She imagined herself writing a few hundred words about a sexy encounter with a Lawrence of Arabia type for one of the women's magazines. Except this wasn't Arabia. And the sexiness was all in the way he looked.

A good hour passed. The sound of explosions coming from below was louder now, if anything. Spasmodic yells and the sound of breaking glass made her shiver. What would Dad have done? Merril asked herself. Would he have skulked up here away from the shooting? The rest of the journalists were holed up in the hotel bar, swapping yarns, all boys together. 'Honestly, Rory,' she had grumbled after breakfast that morning as they'd set off to see what was brewing, 'they seem to expect the stories to come to them! Our papers send us out here in good faith to go out and report on what's happening, not to sit in the bar getting drunk.'

'Perhaps they're scared of getting shot at,' he had suggested expressionlessly.

'Of course they are! They're a bunch of yellow-livered cowards. My father would have been ashamed to call himself a journalist, working with a bunch like that!'

Soon after that they had run into trouble and got separated. She hoped Rory was all right and coming up with some brilliant photos. Impatient to be off, she got up and walked quietly over to the door.

'Don't try it.'

She gave a start, the hoarse voice, full of command, pulling her up like a whiplash. 'I thought you were asleep.' Giving a shrug, she poked her head out. After what had already happened she should have been prepared for the hand that emerged rapidly from within the folds of the scarf, dragging her roughly back inside the portico. 'I'm a free agent,' she protested. 'I do what I like!'

'Not when I'm around you don't. I know this place better than you and I know when it's safe and when it's not, so you'll do exactly as you're told. Understand?'

Merril was about to flare up when she thought better of it. '*Do* you know this place better than me?' she asked.'

'Yes.'

There was a pause, but he didn't take the bait. 'You don't give much away, do you?' she laughed, not feeling amused at all.

He gave a glance outside, looking up at the sky before turning back to her. 'They'll be finished in an hour.' She managed to discern a small frown and he shrugged. 'Then you'll have to wait till dark and we'll try to get you back through the lines to your friends.' There was an odd inflection in his voice, but Merril was too preoccupied to take much notice.

'In England,' she told him, 'I would probably slap your face if you tried to boss me around and interfere with my work like this.'

He gave her an amused look that sent a spiral of fear up her spine. 'But this isn't England . . .' he said softly, letting his words trail away significantly. He noticed the look of uncertainty cross her face at once and, reaching out, he put a friendly hand on her shoulder. 'I'd hate anything to happen to you. Heroics aren't necessary. You can learn far more by treading softly.'

She felt his touch through the thin cotton of her T-shirt like a brand of flame on her flesh, and it was followed by a sudden flooding warmth in her cheeks.

'Heavens!' A hand flew to her face. 'I can't remember ever doing that before——'

'Hard-bitten journalist blushes at man's touch. Headlines, indeed,' he mocked. There was a brief stillness, then slowly he let the offending hand slide away. 'Are you frightened of me?'

She bore the scrutiny of his golden eyes for a moment before answering as honestly as she could, 'No, I don't think so. You probably saved my life down there—and again crossing the piazza.' Even now it hadn't properly sunk in. 'I feel a little bit confused,' she confessed. Her eyes opened wide in amusement and this time there was no guile in her expression. 'None of the home rules seem to apply out here. It's a shock to meet somebody like you.'

Her eyes shone. 'I always knew men like you existed somewhere. You're like my dad——'

'Who?'

'He was a war correspondent, one of the best, always where the action was thickest—a real swashbuckling hero type, just like you——' Merril broke off. He was looking somehow angry, and his eyes had narrowed. When he spoke, his already hoarse voice had roughened even more.

'The real men around here, and the real women, come to that, are the ones who stay put. They live out every day of their lives faced by terrible grinding poverty, struggling to wrest a living from the soil for their children's sake. They're the real heroes. We come and we go. It's easy for us. If things get tough we simply jet out, back to so-called civilisation. No problem.' He gave her a sharp glance. 'You want to meet some real heroes and heroines?'

He sounded genuinely angry and she said, 'I'm sorry. Have I said something wrong?'

'You're suffering from culture shock. Just don't go around making snap judgements about people.'

'I have to. It's my job. There's no time to give everything the in-depth treatment.'

'Journalists!' His tone was scathing. 'You cause more harm than good. You come to places like this, knowing nothing of the people or their problems, stirring up trouble wherever you go. You spend your time sniffing around for stories, and if you don't find any you make them up. Why don't you tell it the way it is for once?'

'That's what I try to do,' she said stiffly. 'I'm not responsible for what other journalists write. But the local people don't make it easy for us. They won't speak to us, they don't want us here. You can't blame us if the reports we file are on the wrong tack if we never get a chance to talk to the people involved.'

'Do you want to meet the people at the top? The so-called rebels?'

Merril looked at him in astonishment. 'Of course I do. But how could you help?'

He put his head on one side and gave her that electric smile again. 'I can help—so long as you don't complain when the going gets tough.'

'What do you mean?'

He took her by the arm. 'Come and sit down—it's not worth the risk to break from here just yet. Trust me. I'll get you a story that'll make headlines. And that's a promise.'

They sat down in the protection of a corner of the building. Reaching up to the cloth around his head, he began to unknot it, revealing his face for the first time, and Merril gave an audible gasp.

'Look a mess, do I?' He grinned and ran the fingers of both hands through his hair, pushing it impatiently back out of his eyes. Merril could only stare. 'Mess' was the last word she would have used. He was beautiful. Like a blond god. The wicked honey-gold eyes were matched by a shock of streaky blond hair, long, wild as a pirate king's, and his blond stubble was the sort any pop celebrity would pay the earth for. She could only gape at him, feeling foolish, unable to think straight. Luckily his head was bent, so he missed her reaction, and by the time he looked up again she had pulled herself together enough to be able to give him a wry smile. 'You had me fooled,' she said shakily. 'You really are English.'

''Fraid so. Were you expecting someone more exotic?'

'Oh, I guess you'll do,' she replied with an air of nonchalance that was all façade. The dazed feeling came back agin, and she closed her eyes.

'Right,' he eventually stood up, 'are you ready?'

'What—what for?' she demanded, trembling slightly.

'I thought you wanted to meet the so-called rebels? Or did you think it was all hot air?'

'I—but——' she stammered, still not quite believing him.

'What's your name?' he asked.

'Merril Park. What's yours?' she riposted, pulling herself together.

'And your paper is——?'

'*News and Views*,' she lifted her chin. 'But——'

'Merril——' He savoured the sound. 'OK, Merril Park of *News and Views*, let's go!'

She was blazingly conscious of his touch again as he pulled her to her feet, and she followed in a daze as far as the door before wrenching herself free and asking, 'But where are we really going?' Suddenly she was frightened. She was alone in a strange country with a man she had only just met. Anything could happen and no one would ever know.

He noticed the flicker of fear in her eyes at once, because he swung back and stood in the doorway with his eyes crinkling in what was becoming a familiar bantering smile.

'There's no danger as long as you stay with me. Do you trust me?'

She held his glance. 'Yes, I trust you.' She knew it was true.

'All I ask is that you promise to write it up honestly.'

'Of course I shall!' she replied at once, insulted to be asked such a thing.

He held out a hand. 'Then let's not waste any more time.'

'But not even you can go marching straight into rebel HQ——' she broke in. As soon as the words were uttered she realised he was the type who would walk in anywhere he wanted.

'I warned you about making snap judgements.' His

eyes held a wicked gleam as he watched her work it out.

'You mean—but you can't——You're not fighting for the rebels——?' Merril gaped at him just as she had done when he'd removed his head-cloth, but this time he was observing her reaction with a wide grin.

'I'm not fighting for anyone. This whole thing can be sorted out by negotiation if everybody will put their guns down long enough.'

'But you're involved with the rebels——' she gasped.

'You make me feel as if I've got two heads,' he laughed. 'Now, do you want to meet them or not? They'll be closing the garrison at sunset.'

Thoughts of the news editor waiting for her story came flooding back. Too bad if she was walking into danger, she would have to do it. When she looked back at her companion she knew that if she was going to be safe with anyone it would be with this tall, blond, ruffianly, widely grinning Englishman.

'There's one condition,' she informed him slowly.

'You're not in a position to impose conditions——' he objected.

'Not even if it's only to ask your name?' she smiled up at him, eyes wide, blue as the sky.

He tweaked a strand of hair from off her cheek. 'Merril——' his husky voice gave her name new meaning and she thrilled to the sound '—you drive a hard bargain.' He paused. 'Call me Azur.' He turned abruptly to the door.

Hurrying after him, she called, 'That's not quite what I meant. I asked for your name, not some alias——' And before he could object again she added, 'But I suppose it'll have to do—for now!'

The next few hours passed rapidly in a whirl of colour and noise. Whether it was due to tiredness or simply culture shock as Azur suggested, Merril felt all she could do was drift with whatever happened next. It was disorientating to feel that she had put herself entirely into someone else's hands, for she had always striven to hold on to her independence, even when she knew it was foolish to do so. But Azur had that effect on her and, rebel or not, she knew she could trust him.

When she walked into the hotel around lunch time the next day she caused a major sensation. As she struggled through the crowd of journalists, it took all her self-control to parry the questions they flung at her without giving anything away. Rory, her photographer, came shouldering his way towards her, a smile of relief all over his face.

'Am I glad to see you!' he exclaimed. 'London hasn't been off the line since I told them you'd gone missing.' He looked her over. 'You look like a cat that's got the cream.'

'And I have, Rory, and I have!' Petite, blonde, and clad in a simple denim jacket and jeans, Merril looked like anything but a red-hot news reporter, but she gave him a ragamuffin smile, big blue eyes alight. 'I feel a bit worse for wear, but I'm all in one piece.'

'Come on, we'll go up to your room and you can tell me all about it,' suggested Rory, taking her by the arm.

She stepped back. 'No, first I ring London.' She noticed his surprise with satisfaction. 'I have a story to file, Rory. The sort commonly known as a scoop!'

Together they went into the communications room, leaving their rivals outside glumly surveying the closed door.

'Ray?' she asked as soon as she got through. 'I've got something for you. It's big.' Then she proceeded to tell the news editor of the paper she worked for what had happened. It was clear he, like everyone else, had assumed she had been kidnapped by the guerillas in the mountainous region north of Kirkuk.

Rory listened in, and when she finished he was smiling. 'You certainly hit the hot spots! Who was this Azur, then? An Englishman, you say?'

'I want a shower, a meal and a drink, in that order. Then we talk,' Merril told him firmly. Rory, five years her senior and an experienced press photographer, let her take over. He rubbed a hand over his sandy-coloured beard as she briefly quoted from her notebook what the rebel leader had told her that morning in the brief meeting Azur had managed to fix for her.

'It's a rum go, all right. But this Azur,' he returned doggedly to the same theme, 'who is he? How did he get to be a mediator between the two factions?'

'His people were out here when he was a child and he lived in the region until he was old enough to go to school in England,' she replied shortly, not wishing to go too deeply into that side of her escapade. She stretched and yawned.

'You can't sleep now. We've got to catch the next flight out.'

'But——' She thought longingly of her bed.

'All foreign journalists are to be out by midnight. It looks as if this thing is going to be bigger than we first thought.' Rory patted her on the shoulder. 'You'll get all the sleep you need on the flight. We're being sent via Rome.'

It was raining as they circled Heathrow next morning after spending an uncomfortable night at Rome airport and taking the first available flight on to London. The plane drifted down through layers of cotton-wool cloud graded like a colour chart, gradually darkening the lower they dropped. At ground level the runway gleamed like smoked glass. People were hunched forward, ducking into the upturned collars of raincoats as they hurried between airport building and bus.

The scene couldn't have been more different from the one Merril was carrying inside her head, the one nobody yet knew about. It was of a certain hillside at dawn, made lovely by the belling of goats on the hills, cicadas, the scent of wild thyme and . . . She shook herself and tried to concentrate.

A car had been sent from the paper and there was a message to go straight in to see the chief himself. It was only half-past two as the car crawled through the crowded London streets and eventually pulled up outside the offices in Fleet Street. To Merril it seemed like another century.

Ray Doyle came puffing excitedly round his desk the minute she came in through the glass doors of the news room. 'You little peach—I knew you could do it! I've always put my faith in you, you darling. I hope you appreciate it.'

'Yes, Ray,' she replied wearily. She was surprised to see that things looked much the same as when she and Rory had left. In only two days she felt as if her world had been turned upside-down.

'She's tired,' Rory said protectively.

'Of course she is.' Ray tried to pat her on the shoulder, but such gestures were alien to him and something in Merril's expression made him drop his hand. 'Come on through, the big man's waiting.'

Merril stifled a sigh. They were back with a vengeance now, back to the old hierarchy, the pecking order in which she was bottom of the line.

Ushered into the carpeted office of the chief editor, she was congratulated on filing a first-class story, though. It was uplifting to feel she was being noticed for what she herself had done and not, as usual, because of her father's fame. She had pipped everyone else at the post, even the foreign dailies who were notoriously tough in that part of the world.

'I don't know how you did it,' the chief beamed.

'By being in the right place at the right time,' replied Merril, quoting her father. She wasn't so jet-lagged that she didn't see the looks the three men exchanged.

Later she went back to the flat to unwind. Her flatmate Annie worked on a fashion magazine and arrived home just as Merril was coming out of the shower.

'Darling, you're back! I was so worried. Damian phoned me and told me what had happened—he was demented, poor dear! Your whole office was in an uproar.'

'Damian, demented?' Merril wrapped a big pink towel round herself and flopped down in an armchair.

'Have you eaten?' Annie gave her a sharp glance. 'When did you get in? Have you been into the office? What did Ray say? I bet that was one in the eye for him. Darling, you look all in. What can I get you?'

'I feel rather fragile. London doesn't seem real.' Merril was used to Annie. Despite the fashionable elegance of her manner, all gloss and Titian good looks, she had the proverbial heart of gold and proved it now by bustling around fixing drinks. 'Here,' she said, 'you enjoy this while I get some food on the go. When did you last eat?'

'Yesterday, I think. Or was it today? I really can't remember.'

While Annie cut and sliced in the kitchen, refusing any offer of help with a sharp slap as Merril tried to join in, she repeated what she had already said about Damian, adding, 'Have you seen him yet?'

Merril shook her head. 'He hadn't crossed my

mind. And when you say demented, I think that's
usual, isn't it?'

'Mean child! He's quite mad about you.'

'Oh, dear. It would take something like my going
missing for twenty-four hours to spoil a beautiful and
so far undemanding friendship.'

'A theatre critic might be quite fun.' Annie gave her
a sharp glance.

'As husband material?'

'Well, why not?'

'But I'm not looking, Annie. Please! Not just now. I
haven't come down to earth yet.' This was their one
bone of contention. Annie had a lot of men-friends,
but they were only friends and nothing more because
they had been quickly relegated to the unsuitable-as-
husband category. She couldn't understand why
Merril wasn't as practical, and tried to help out by
vetting Merril's men for her when she got the chance.
It was always done in a spirit of helpfulness, and
Merril usually hadn't the heart to resist, knowing that
when it came to it she would do the choosing herself.

'It'd be like you to fall for this rebel chief,' Annie
muttered now, slicing carrots and tipping them into a
casserole with her usual dexterity. She happened to
glance up just then and caught Merril's expression.
'Darling! I was only joking . . .'

Merril pulled herself together. 'You're barking up
the wrong tree as usual, Annie. The rebel chief—and
when you read my piece about him I hope you'll start
calling him the opposition leader—must have been
about eighty if he was a day. A lovely man, but
definitely not husband material, not even in my
book.'

'Then what was that strange, rather far-away
expression on your face when I happened to look up
just now?'

'Your imagination.' Merril averted her face and

began to busy herself with the gin and tonic Annie had thrust into her hands.

'And how long have we shared a flat?'

'You're a horrible witch, Annie. You haven't been in the flat five minutes and already you think you've sussed me out!' Merril lifted her face in a last attempt at subterfuge. 'How on earth could I meet and fall for someone in less than twenty-four hours?'

'It need only take seconds. The secret glance across a crowded room.'

'You certainly have the right job. I suppose that's the sort of stuff you sell your readers. "Darlings, wait for that magic moment when his eyes meet yours——" '

'So I *am* right. How exciting! Is he one of the journalists? One of the French ones?' Annie put down her knife and smiled infuriatingly at Merril's upturned face.

'When I've put some clothes on and had a taste of this concoction you're throwing together,' she replied with dignity, 'then, possibly, I might just have something to tell you . . . Trouble is, I can predict exactly what you're going to say—"not good husband material, darling"—well,' Merril stood in the doorway, 'you can guess what I'll say to that!'

It was Annie with the phone in her hand who woke her. 'It's for you.' She threw the receiver on to the bed where Merril could reach it.

She must have gone out like a light. Struggling to sit up, she darted out a hand, then let it freeze as she woke fully. Her heart dropped like a ton of bricks. She had been dreaming she was back in the hotel room in the Kirkuk mountains, and for one wild minute had imagined it was a certain husky-voiced 'rebel' on the line . . . Regaining her composure, she took the call, knowing even before he spoke that it was Damian. She let him rattle on for a few minutes, then made her excuses. Later, in fresh jumper and skirt, hair washed and dried, she went to join Annie in the living-room where the table was already set. She didn't need any invitation to launch into a detailed account of her meeting with Azur.

'It was exactly what you're always talking about, Annie,' she began. 'Eyes across a crowded room. Except that in this case it was a street full of gunmen. And I only noticed his eyes when he dragged me to safety in an empty house.'

'How exciting! So the rumours were all true? You were kidnapped?'

Merril shook her head. Then with a deep breath she began to tell Annie what had happened, only letting her words trail away when the official part of her story came to an end.

Annie gave her a sidelong look. 'But then what happened?' she demanded. 'You must have spent the night with him——?'

'It's true, we had to stay in hiding until nightfall, then we walked for hours into the hills. He took me to a ruined farm and we slept for a few hours——' Merril shot a disparaging look at the expression on Annie's face. 'I know what you're thinking. And yes, it could have been tricky—but I knew he was totally trustworthy. I've already told you that——'

'But you've also admitted you fancied each other——'

Annie's words didn't do justice to the way Merril felt about Azur. She recalled the night, the silence of the countryside, the sliver of moon that slipped slowly from one side of the open window to the other. Sunrise.

She knew she was hooked. There had been something powerful between them from the very first. His outrageous good looks were simply a bonus

—wicked honey-gold eyes, that shock of streaky blond hair, long, rough, wild, that electrifying smile . . .

She gave a shaky laugh. 'I don't know what's happening to me. I've never fallen for anyone like this before. And it's all so hopeless, isn't it? I don't even know his real name. He was very definite—no biographies. It works both ways. All he knows about me is my name and the paper I work for.'

'But the night,' prompted Annie, 'what about the night?'

Merril was lost in thought for a moment, then she gave a rueful smile. 'It wasn't like you imagine. I told you, I knew I could trust him—in every way.' When Annie gave a knowing little smile, she went on, 'He showed me a sort of hay-filled mattress thing in one of the rooms. ''We'll have to sleep on that,'' he said. ''If you're worried, we can put a knife between us—like the sword between Tristan and Iseult . . .'' of course I trusted him.'

Suddenly she found hot tears gushing from her eyes, and Annie put a friendly arm around her shoulders.

'There, there,' she comforted. 'You've been through an awful lot. You need a good hot meal and nice long rest. I hope Ray Doyle has given you the rest of the week off?'

'Of course he hasn't. He'd better not—I don't want Mike Davis stealing my story.' Merril stifled a sob. 'I suppose you're right, though—a meal and bed would be nice.'

Merril expected things to get back to normal fairly soon after this. After all, it had only been a job, more exciting than the usual routine stuff, but if she was going to prove herself she couldn't let her feelings get in the way.

As the days passed, though, she found it increasingly difficult to settle back into the old routine. Everywhere she looked she saw loving couples wrapped in each other's arms, and she longed to be with Azur again, to see that bantering smile light up his face.

Confessing all this to Annie one evening, she said, 'I'm sick of the office. I think I'll resign.'

'Don't be crazy, darling! You feel restless, that's all. It'll pass. You'll get used to being back.'

'Oh, Annie, why don't they have men like Azur over here? I'm sick of wimps and wallies. What's happened to all the real men?'

'I know a handful,' said Annie, considering. 'Well, one or maybe even two . . .' She gave a brilliant smile. 'I'll work on that one. Trust me!'

As the days became one week, then two, Merril's restlessness turned in on itself, until one day she simply let rip at the nearest person and there was a huge row in the middle of the office. Ray Doyle intervened.

'Take two days off—that's an order. I want you to go to the Chelsea Flower Show when you get back.'

'Oh, don't be ridiculous, Ray!' She stared at him as if he were mad.

'Somebody's got to cover it,' he told her, looking as tough as his balding head and paunch would allow.

To his immense mystification, his top girl news reporter immediately burst into floods of tears.

Later Merril mentioned the incident to Annie. 'It's what Azur predicted—the Chelsea Flower Show and man bites dog stories. Oh, Annie, I'll never forget him!'

'You certainly won't so long as you keep going on about him. I'm supposed to be the romantic one of us two, don't forget.'

Merrill had the grace to blush. 'I can't help it. I know I'll never meet anyone like him again.'

Annie shrugged. 'Suit yourself. But at least warn off the lovesick swains. Speaking of which, Damian rang. You left the office without finalising the arrangements for tonight.'

'Damn tonight. Did I say I'd go out with him?'

'You did indeed. Surely you haven't forgotten? It's the first night of that new play everybody's raving about.'

'How can they be raving if it's the first night?' Merril retorted as she got up to get ready.

'Because it did phenomenal business in the provinces and it's coming into the West End to take us all by storm, that's how.'

'It won't take *me* by storm. I'm not in the mood for cardboard cut-outs.' She came to the bathroom door. 'Actors, huh! I'd rather curl up in front of the TV and watch the news.''

'And dream of him, I suppose,' said Annie drily.

By the time the doorbell rang Merril had grudgingly submitted to Annie's blandishments and put up her hair, donning a shocking pink taffeta dress from out of Annie's special collection. 'It *is* a first night,' she reproved when Merril was about to throw on any old thing.

She liked nothing better than to dress people up. First she made Merril try on a slinky black draped affair with an off-the-shoulder neckline and tiny beaded flowers round the hem. Then she changed her mind and insisted that she try on the taffeta. 'Sensational' was her verdict. 'That should make Damian's hair curl!'

'God forbid!' grumbled Merril. 'I'm not in the mood for theatrical types. Damian's really over the top sometimes when he gets backstage.'

'I thought you felt it was all rather fun?'

'All that false enthusiasm, false smiles, false hair, false eyelashes—and that's only the men. Why are you making me suffer, Annie? Will you go instead?' For a moment Merril looked hopeful.

'Nonsense. I'm seeing Cornel.'

'Again? Oh well, here goes,' said Merril resignedly as she made her departure.

Despite the good-natured bantering she felt strangely disembodied, as if everything going on around her was only the interval between two acts of a play. The first act had been the meeting with Azur, but what the second was going to be she couldn't imagine.

Damian was sweet. He was everything a girl could want in an escort, as Annie reminded Merril in a whispered aside just before she left.

Tonight he was impeccably turned out in dinner-jacket and blood-red carnation, dark hair fashionably groomed, and a slight though artificial tan setting off his ready smile; he was quite the most presentable male in the office. Not quite six feet and rather narrow in the shoulder, he should have made her heart flutter just a little, Merril pondered, especially when, having settled her comfortably in his sleek black car and flicked on the lush stereo, he ran a sensual finger over the back of her hand, murmuring, 'I'm so glad you said yes, darling. I've missed you.'

She withdrew her hand unobtrusively from beneath his, as if to readjust her seat-belt. 'Missed me? I've been sitting across the office from you every day for goodness knows how long!'

'Missed you ever since you went on that foreign assignment, I mean. It's as if you haven't quite come back to me——' He paused, his sensitive face full of concern. 'Before you left we seemed to be growing close, but now——'

'Aren't you going to start the car? We'll be late,

won't we?'

'Merril, we're not going to get another chance to be alone for the rest of the evening, and at work we don't seem to have time to talk much these days. I do care about what's happening to us——'

'Oh, for heaven's sake, Damian, can't we just enjoy ourselves? I don't want to get into some heavy emotional scene tonight!'

She felt guilty to see his eyes darken with hurt for a moment, then he gave a light laugh. 'No, even I can see that! We play it for laughs, then, do we? As long as you're sure that's what you want.' He patted her hand, trying to hide his evident disappointment at her lack of warmth, and with an air of resignation turned the key in the ignition.

Soon they were entering the crowded foyer of the West End theatre where the first night was to be held.

Merril's preoccupation with Azur over the last two weeks had hidden from her the fact that there was a new excitement on the scene. Damian's job as theatre critic kept him in the forefront of showbiz gossip, but Merril had failed to take in that tonight was one of those special nights rumoured to be a landmark in theatre first nights. In its out-of-town run the show had been a smash hit, a fact that had totally escaped her.

Now the splendid gold and green foyer was thronged with well-known faces, flashbulbs kept up a continuous lightning attack as one after another the already famous came to pay court to a star in the making. One actor, Damian told her, had pulled the show from out of its original rating as just another moderately good crowd-puller, his name now on everyone's lips. It was all news to Merril.

She pulled at Damian's arm as they drifted with the crowd beneath the magnificent central chandelier towards the main house. 'Just tell me, Damian,' she whispered, '*who* is this genius we've all come to see?'

He raised his eyebrows. 'Really, Merril, don't let anybody hear you say that, you'd never live it down! He's the latest *cause célèbre*. An absolutely brilliant discovery called Torrin Anthony.'

Merril looked critically round at the over-made-up, avid, eager faces of the many older women in their expensive clothes, as they cooed and brayed at each other over the bald heads of their escorts. 'Some new toy boy, by the look of things,' she said bitchily. 'What a bore!'

'Not at all. He's in his early thirties.'

'Then if he's so wonderful, why haven't we heard of him before now?'

'He's one of these dedicated types who nurse their talent, picking and choosing parts he really wants to play. It means he's frequently been out of work or playing in obscure provincial theatres with directors he's wanted to work with, rather than going for the big, glamorous showcase roles. He avoids publicity and refuses to be interviewed or even have his photo released——'

'Oh, how pretentious! And to be able to act in this high-minded way no doubt he has a nice rich family to support him, too!' For some reason Merril was determined to dislike everything she heard about this man. The hullabaloo in the foyer was deafening, cries of 'darling!' and 'sweetie!' irritating her as they had never done before.

Damian took her by the arm. 'You usually find this scene fun,' he remarked. 'That's why I thought you'd enjoy being here tonight.' He held one of her hands in his. 'I thought it might remind you of old times, but instead it looks as if I've made a gaffe.'

'I'm sorry, Damian—am I being too beastly?' She was shamefaced. 'I don't seem to be able to get in the mood for anything much these days.'

For a moment Damian pulled her close, one arm slipping lightly around her waist. She couldn't move away because people were surging around them, going in to find their seats. 'If it's anything you want to talk about, you know I'm always available——'

'I'm sorry, Damian,' she put up a hand and let it rest on his shoulder for a moment, 'I don't know what's got into me. I'll try to enjoy the show. It's really lovely to be here.'

Even as she said it she knew it sounded horribly false, but it couldn't be unsaid. She knew she was going to hate every minute of the next few hours.

They took their seats near the front of the stalls. One thing about Damian, Merril thought as she looked round at her extravagantly dressed neighbours, his job meant he could always come up with the best seats in the house, and vanity made her glad she had allowed Annie to make her wear the shocking pink taffeta. Then her thoughts were interrupted by the rising of the curtain, and silence fell.

As she watched the unfolding scenes, something strange started to happen. It was as if the audience was holding its breath until Torrin Anthony made his entrance. And then—then even Merril felt them fall as one under his spell.

Tall, dark, handsome—and with a too, too predictable appeal, was her verdict as she watched. But the audience had a different view. She tried to fight it, ignore it, but, critical though she was, she couldn't help but be aware, like them, of the man's charisma. She sneaked a glance from time to time along the row of faces on each side. Everyone was transfixed. Not a shuffle or a cough broke the rapt attention with which they hung on his every word and gesture.

The play was a sort of eighteenth-century tragicomedy, with songs and clowning and all kinds of theatrical effects, but the way it was played gave it a contemporary significance, and Merril could see why it had caught everyone's imagination.

During the interval she grudgingly admitted to Damian that she was beginning to get an inkling of what all the fuss was about, though as far as she was concerned the man was a sham and had simply made such an impact because it was a peach of a role.

'You're the only woman in the place who wouldn't sell her soul to the devil for him.' He paused, eyeing her flushed and haughty face with some amusement. 'Though I'm delighted to hear you're so impervious to his rather rakish charm. When I come to write my review I shall make a special note of it.'

'But he is all show, isn't he?' Surely you can see that?' she burst out. 'That calculated slightly world-weary cynicism, with just a hint of the master crook about him.'

'He lookes well in brocade. Surely you'll give him that?'

'Oh, very well,' she admitted with a deprecating laugh. 'A proper Regency rake. A pirate, in fact, with that dark glossy hair in a pigtail—very contemporary. And the padded shoulders——'

'Are they padded?'

'Don't you think so?'

They fell into a discussion of whether or not Torrin Anthony's shoulders were real or not, and a group of Damian's friends joined in with all the frivolity such a subject warranted. Even Merril noticed that the men were relieved there was at least one woman who hadn't gone overboard about him.

'My wife's totally mad about the chap. How can I compete with a Lord Rakewell?' a genial though decidedly paunchy-looking man whose name she had instantly forgotten confided in her as they stood in a circle beside the bar.

Someone else chipped in. 'It's because nobody knows anything about him—that's my theory. Women love a mystery, don't you know?'

'Yes, just wait until he has a profile in the press. It'll be like bursting a bubble. Once they find out he likes two fried eggs with his bacon and went to Eton, the mystery will evaporate and we'll all be able to relax——'

'He's no doubt counting on it, that's why he refuses to give interviews. We've been after him for months, but his agent, bless her, won't even let us speak to him on the telephone. Keeps his phone number ex-directory and his address a total secret.'

'Doesn't want your foot-in-the-door techniques, old boy. Can't say I blame her.'

'As if we would!' The journalist thus addressed smiled into his brandy. 'I'd like to pull off an interview soon, though, before anybody else gets in on it.'

'Send a pretty girl along. What about Merril here?' The men turned to look at her.

'You must be joking!' she laughed. 'I'm a news journalist, not a showbiz gossip columnist!'

'Tactless, sweetheart, very tactless,' whispered Damian in her ear as they went back to their seats. 'You've just turned down an offer from one of the top features editors in the country.'

'I don't care,' Merril told him as she settled in her seat. 'Torrin Anthony is the last man on earth I want to interview.'

Her opinion was confirmed later at the backstage party.

'Oh, Damian, do we have to?' she protested when they were finally able to leave their seats after a record number of curtain calls. Those in the know were already flocking backstage.

'Look you know I have to phone in my crit straight away. You may as well join the admiring throng for a few minutes.'

'Then by the time you get back I'll have changed my mind about partying all night. Oh, very well. I'm sorry I'm such a misery. Best smile—promise!' Merril gave him a peck on the cheek before he went off to phone in his review.

It *is* an occasion, she thought, so I must make an effort to be pleasant—but someone like Azur would loathe all this tinselly nonsense.

She stood by a window at the end of the corridor leading to the dressing-rooms to wait for Damian, but one of his friends came back to look for her with a glass of champagne in his hand.

'Drink this while you're waiting. The party's going to be on stage. We're all in Torrin's dressing-room—you can't miss it.' He pointed to the far end of the corridor, where a crowd was jammed into one of the doorways. He was evidently in a hurry to get back. Equally evidently, Damian had given him the task of chaperoning her. He waited for her halfway back along the corridor.

'Everybody's here tonight,' he told her with satisfaction. 'Isn't this an occasion? That final scene—phew! I don't mind admitting I had tears in my eyes.' He went on in this rather irritating vein all the time they were making their way towards the subdued uproar at the other end, and, trying to conceal her reluctance, Merril made one or two noncommittal noises as she followed him down, already hating the babble of voices, but welcoming the anonymity of the crowd once she felt it immerse her.

There was no asking where Torrin Anthony was—it was obvious. The star was where a star should be, firmly in the centre of things. He hadn't had time to change out of his stage clothes before the crowd of well-wishers descended, and he was lounging in a chair in front of a large lighted mirror, graciously extending a lace-cuffed wrist to receive handshakes of congratulation from the stream of people who came in.

Standing anonymously in the wings, as it were, Merril had a chance to have a good look at him. His eyes, she thought, looked dark with strain, until she remembered he was an actor and this was presumably the image he wanted to create tonight. Every so often the now famous smile would dazzle as he lifted his head to accept the tributes pressed on him. The narrow rake's moustache, she now saw, was simply make-up. Underneath all the goo he would look quite different, and there was no way of knowing what he was really like. Part of his mystique, she judged unkindly. As she studied his face between the bobbing heads of his admirers, Damian appeared beside her.

'Lost your indifference, I see.' He sounded rather sharp.

'Not at all——'

'You were giving him a pretty thorough scrutiny.'

'Wondering what made him tick—and if I could see the cracks in the carefully polished facade.'

Just then there was a slight change in the hum of conversation, and she looked up to see the subject of their exchange staring straight at her. The half dozen people closest to him had noticed the direction of his gaze, and all turned to look at the same moment. There was a lull.

Merril felt a sensation like ice run up her spine and lodge itself somewhere in her throat, so that she would have found it impossible to speak had she so wished. But the initiative was taken from her, for the actor, with studied art, raised one hand and beckoned to her to come over to him.

There was the smile again—rakish, dangerous, confident. His eyes, a lighter brown than she had imagined, were still outlined in dark pencil.

Everyone waited, expecting her to move forward, showing how honoured she was to share the limelight, but something stopped her. Never shy, now she wished the ground would swallow her up. It was as if he expected her to say something, to do something—yet all she could do was stare at him while he waited, one hand extended towards her.

'Go on, Merril, get that interview for us,' whispered Damian in her ear. He pushed her in the small of the back.

But she couldn't move and she watched, mesmerised, as Torrin Anthony rose to his feet and slowly came towards her.

He seemed even taller off stage. She was reminded sickeningly of Azur, how he had towered over her when he dragged her to safety into the bombed house. But this man was an actor—even his height seemed put on, as if he had shrugged it on together with that air of authority he had adopted!

She put up a hand as if to ward him off. Everyone was watching.

'Well?' he asked. He was smiling into her eyes, his own now bright, teasing—rake's eyes, assessing a pretty woman. 'So here you are!' He picked up both her hands and, bending his dark head to them, turned them over so that they lay defenceless, palms uppermost, in his own. Then, before she could snatch them away, he placed his lips softly in first one and then in the other.

CHAPTER TWO

HIS DARK head seemed to bend over her hands for an age. She couldn't move and she couldn't speak, she could only watch until at last he raised his head. Still keeping hold of her hands, he simply looked into her eyes without saying anything. The room fell silent.

Afterwards Merril told Annie it was a deliberate attempt to exert his famous charm on the one person present who hadn't already succumbed. But at the time she didn't know what was happening to her. Her mind felt blank, confused. It was ridiculous, like being hypnotised, or as if her entire life had been a dream and this was the only real moment in it. It was what people called 'presence', she supposed, and it was difficult to describe by what seemingly magic art he could make everyone else pale into the background—but it was an actor's trick of the trade, nothing more, a knack he must have picked up at drama school. He'd got it down to a fine art and everyone fell. But not her. Not when she'd sussed out what he was up to.

In the silence around them, which seemed to stretch endlessly, she had time to observe tiny details of his appearance with pinpoint clarity: thick, black eyelashes, sweeping down over pale cheekbones, a dusting of fine powder over them, a trick that failed to hide tiny laugh lines at the corners of his eyes—beginnings of crow's feet, she remarked waspishly later—and designed, without a doubt, to enhance a pale, romantically haunted image, at odds with those kindling amber eyes gazing with such

38

disturbing familiarity into hers.

That he seemed at first surprised by her silence, then amused, did not endear him to her. She felt foolishly out of step. His presence, so intimate that she could smell the exotic spice of cologne mingled with stage make-up, was a physical intrusion, demanding a response she did not want to give.

Before she could remove her hands from his he let them slip away; then, before either of them had a chance to speak, a woman with red hair and a tiny scrap of evening dress, all straps and slits, threw herself into his arms with a shrill, predatory cry.

'Darling! I knew you'd do it. A star is born!' she declaimed to the room full of people. Her arms twined round his neck before he could move, and for a moment the red hair and the sleek black ponytail mingled a few inches from Merril's affronted face.

She stepped hurriedly back to avoid being trampled. Torrin Anthony was already unlocking the woman's arms from around his neck as Merril turned, bumping into Damian who was standing directly behind her, and as she moved away she suddenly regained her voice and her composure at the same time.

'*Do* let's get out of here, Damian. I'm really not in the mood for all this theatrical nonsense,' she said in a loud, deliberately disparaging voice.

Torrin Anthony heard every word, because his head jerked up as if to reply. But, as he warded off his admirer's embrace, Merril, sweeping swiftly out of the room, didn't give him time to utter. The space she left was immediately filled by a wave of fans coming in from the corridor.

Damian caught up with her outside. He was not amused. 'Merril, I don't understand what's got into you—surely you could at least be civil to the man?'

'Being civil doesn't mean dropping at his feet like

everyone else, thanks!'

Despite his remonstrance, a smile of satisfaction flitted across his face. 'So he's not your type, but at least think of the paper.'

'Damn the paper!' To her surprise Merril found she was shaking. She leaned back against the wall and tried to gather her wits. Damian tried to draw her into his arms, but she turned her head and he had to be content with a kiss on the side of her neck.

'I know how desperately you want to go home, darling, and in normal circumstances your wish would be my command, but I'm afraid tonight is out of the ordinary. I *have* to stay for the party. Damn it, I *want* to! Now, if you like I can pop you in a taxi——'

'No, no,' she replied wearily. Whether it was the thought of being 'popped in a taxi', or sheer tiredness, she didn't know, but she shook her head, muttering, 'I'm more stressed than I realised.' She gave him a half-smile. 'I'll stick it out. You know me, never say die! But it is so false, isn't it? All that screaming and blind adulation——'

'He's very good,' Damian reminded her.

'So, he's good! But he's only an actor!' She raised her voice. 'What's so special about that? He's not God almighty!'

Damian had been nuzzling into her shoulder in an attempt to persuade her to stay, when something about his sudden stillness made her turn to follow his glance.

Torrin Anthony had come out of his dressing-room and was standing just a yard away in the act of walking along the corridor towards them, but he too had frozen and now he stood, a somehow unhappy figure in the harsh light of the corridor. The brocade jacket and drooping lace jabot were out of place off stage, and the black liner was beginning to smear in the heat. His eyes were two dark pits focused on

Merril. He looked exhausted.

He must have heard what I just said, she told herself without emotion. It would be a shock to realise that not everyone thought he was Mr Wonderful.

Damian was the first to pull himself together. 'Damian West, *News and Views*,' he said, stepping round Merril's inert body as if it were some fixed obstacle in his way and moving towards Torrin Anthony with a hand outstretched in greeting. Thus addressed, the actor took Damian's hand without seeming to see it, his eyes still fixed on Merril's now haughtily averted face.

'We've tried to contact you several times in the last few weeks,' went on Damian enthusiastically, 'because of course we'd like to fix up an interview as soon as possible while the show's still hot.'

Merril turned to watch as Torrin Anthony shook himself like a man coming out of a dream, then he glanced at Damian, automatically switching on the charm, hundred-watt smile going full blast. 'My agent fixes all that sort of thing. Best if you contact her.'

'Unluckily for us she seems rather keen to protect you from us big bad press boys, and——'

'Oh, yes, she does,' Torrin smiled vaguely, failing to make the connection Damian wanted him to make. His glance returned to Merril who was still standing pressed back slightly against the wall, as if expecting him to try to squeeze past and wanting to put as much distance between them as possible. She found she was actually holding her breath. But he didn't move. He merely stood where he was, as if undecided on his next move.

Poor man, she thought, he's floored without an admiring audience. She was relieved to find Damian still chuntering on about the integrity of his paper and what an honour it would be to be granted an interview. She thought he might even have said 'audience', she told Annie later, such was the obsequiousness of his manner. But it gave her time to pull herself together, and then, just as she was about to walk away, a door opened further down the corridor and a man of about sixty, sprucely rigged out in a light beige suit, came walking blithely towards them.

'Ready for the fray, Torrin, old man——' Then he stopped. 'I say, what's all this? Still in slap?'

As if released from a tableau, Torrin Anthony swivelled. 'The fray is all in my dressing-room. I haven't had a chance to unwind or change or anything——' He looked slightly harassed and held out his hands helplessly.

'Tell 'em to get lost, old boy. A chap needs a bit of privacy after a performance like that. Chuck 'em out. Come on, I'll help you.'

'Don't do that,' said Torrin Anthony quickly, but he gave a look as if he'd like nothing better than to turf out the lot of them bodily. 'I'll come down as I am. I shan't be staying long.'

Turning his back on the milling crowd by now spilling out into the corridor in full cry after him, he put a friendly arm round the other man's shoulders and began to walk off down the corridor in the direction of the stage. Before he reached the corner he turned back to where Damian and Merril were still standing—watching, said Merril afterwards, as if we were at a private performance, all eyes on the star—and called back, 'You're very welcome to the party. Do come along!'

'Do you think he'll bite?' asked Damian when he'd gone.

'Bite?' Merril looked at him with an image of Torrin Anthony's flawless white teeth swamping her thoughts until it dawned on her that Damian was still fussing about his interview. 'Oh, I expect so. Even Garbo didn't avoid *all* publicity, did she?' She went up to Damian and patted his cheek. 'He needs us more than we need him, Damian. Don't you worry.'

She allowed him to lead her backstage, stumbling after him in the half-dark over the debris of pulleys and coiled ropes and flimsy props that seemed to have been flung down anywhere in the narrow space behind the scenes. It was an odd feeling to walk on to the set of an eighteenth-century coaching inn after sitting gazing at it for so long from beyond the footlights. Everything seemed slightly out of scale, and it fostered Merril's increasing sense of unreality.

She leaned against a solid-looking piece of furniture, only to find it slide away beneath her.

'Steady, don't smash the set,' a voice reproved. It was the actor who had greeted Torrin Anthony earlier. He was by himself, and she remembered his face from countless television series. He wandered off towards a makeshift bar erected nearby.

The stage soon filled with a milling throng of what she privately alluded to as 'theatrical types'. The noise seemed unbearable. Everyone seemed to be on intimate terms with everyone else. Torrin Anthony's impossibly black hair, surely dyed, was visible now and then in the crowd that constantly surrounded him.

Damian had thrust himself into the thick of it all, tending his contacts, enjoying the backstage gossip, but Merril resolutely hung around by herself on the fringes. She couldn't wait to get away from it all, back home to watch the late movie and dream once more and undisturbed of Azur.

Before she could safely ask Damian to drive her back there were speeches to be got through, champagne, toasts to a long and successful run.

Nobody doubted that the show was going to be a raving success. There was frantic applause, more champagne. Then suddenly someone was calling for the star.

She watched from a perch at the side as hands thrust him to the front, hoisting him on to a platform so he could be seen. From her vantage point she could observe him as clearly as if she were behind the scenes, every little gesture visible. She saw how tightly his hands were clenched, partly concealed within the folds of his coat. When she looked at his face, she again saw something like strain in the dark eyes, masked quickly beneath an air of nonchalance as he swung his head to take in the whole crowd in front of him. There was a hush, the partying stopping like magic as everyone waited for him to speak. But the silence lengthened. There was a cough or two, a quickly hushed clink of glasses.

Her eyes swivelled back to him. Wearing a full-sleeved cambric shirt cut in a flowing eighteenth-century style, lace jabot unfastened to reveal an arrow slit of tanned torso where the white stage make-up ended, he had the demeanour of a French *aristo* about to make his guillotine speech. Merril cast a quick glance from the powerful shoulders to the brocade jacket. Even to her critical eye, it was obvious he didn't need shoulder pads. Then she watched more closely still as the silence unexpectedly continued.

A wag from the cast called, 'He's dried!' and there was a round of good-natured applause, while somebody else added, 'Better now than in the court speech!'

It's true, registered Merril in surprise. He doesn't know what to say. She watched as he slowly managed to pull himself together, and as the laughter died away he seemed to take several deep breaths before saying quietly in a voice like velvet, 'You're absolutely right.' The electrifying smile lit his face for a moment and he went on, 'As everyone knows who works with me, I'm quite useless without a script.' He lowered his head. At once everyone was on his side.

Merril gawped in disbelief. They really fell for it! People actually believed this little performance! As if an actor of his experience and skill would be scared at the prospect of getting up among a group of friends and saying a few lines of thanks! Couldn't people see it was his way of getting them to eat out of his hand?

With an expression of sheer disbelief on her face, she listened to him finish. It's like an awards ceremony, she thought from her perch—compliments all round, shallow flattery for all. And all so sickeningly false.

'Aren't we all too, too modest, dahling!' she murmured to Damian who rejoined her a few minutes later. But Torrin Anthony's hesitation, the fleeting look of panic on his face as he turned to face that sea of people without a script in his hand, wouldn't leave her. She had to hand it to him—it had been beautifully convincing.

After the speeches, the toasts and the euphoria at the certainty of a long run, the music and the dancing started, and Torrin Anthony, all 'stagefright' forgotten, became a black-haired dervish with a never ending succession of eye-catching partners.

'Let's go,' suggested Damian once it became obvious he wasn't going to get any further with the question of an interview.

'Best thing you've said all evening,' replied Merril, adding with uncharacteristic rancour before she could stop herself, 'I, for one, have had enough of the empty charm of Torrin Anthony.'

*   *   *

Next morning she had to interview an MP at his office in Westminster. It took her twice as long as usual to get back to the office, and the first person she met was Ray Doyle, who barked, 'I thought I told you to take two days off?'

'So you can give my story to Mike, I suppose?' She glanced over at the empty desk where her main competitor usually sat. She had written up the piece about the foreign conflict and Azur's key role as mediator, but there had been so many repurcussions from it, even though the two sides were now reconciled, she felt she had to stick around to field whatever else came up. Besides, there was always a faint chance that Azur would try to contact her . . .

'Don't talk nonsense, woman. Mike's got his hands full with some city scandal. Here, let me see that piece you've got there.'

'Give me a chance, Ray! I know I'm Superwoman, but you want it written up nicely, don't you?'

Merril felt she could take liberties these days, and sauce was something Ray seemed able to cope with, as if he felt it defined her femininity more clearly than even the blonde curls and blue eyes.

'You twist me round your little finger,' he grumbled, 'but don't think I don't mean it. I don't want to see you in this office until——' he glanced across at the wall calendar '—next Monday morning.'

'But that's nearly five days!'

'Including today and the weekend, yes, it is.'

'What's the opposite of a slavedriver?' she flung at him as he made his way between the desks. She was already going through her messages as she spoke, and she stopped then with a memo in her hand. Damian was sitting at his typewriter on the far side of the room, and she called across, 'Here! This must be meant for you.'

Ray gave her a warning look from the door of his office

and Damian, fingers still pounding the keys, glanced across at her.

'It's your invitation to meet the great man himself—at least, you're to call his agent.'

'What?' Damian looked up.

'Message from Sally Hamilton, agent to the star of the moment, Torrin Anthony. Please call me, it says. Here, it must be for you.'

Damian rose to his feet and almost snatched the scrap of paper from out of her hand. 'Quick off the mark.' He could barely conceal his pleasure.

As she went back to her own desk and began to busy herself with notes she had taken that morning, Merril heard Damian pick up his phone straight away. Absorbed by her task, she wasn't aware of anything else until she felt a tap on her shoulder. Looking rather miffed, Damian held out the memo. 'It was for you, after all. So I'm informed.'

'Me?' She looked at the scribbled message again. It had come in that morning at eleven-fifteen and her name was pencilled in clearly enough. 'But obviously there's some mistake——' she began.

'Not according to Miss Hamilton.'

'What the dickens does she mean by contacting me? Does she imagine I'm interested in theatre?'

'Have to ask her yourself,' replied Damian somewhat stiffly, and stalked back to his desk.

Pushing the matter to the back of her mind, Merril returned to her work, but it was difficult to concentrate now. She rewrote the same sentence three times, then gave up and dialled the number she had been given.

A husky voice answered at the other end when she got past Reception, and as soon as she knew she was speaking to Miss Hamilton herself she launched into an explanation. 'Obviously there's been some mistake. I handle hard news, not——' She broke off, not wishing to sound too disparaging.

'So I understand,' came the reply, helping her over the difficulty with a deep-throated chuckle, 'but Mr Anthony is being absolutely hounded by the press, as you can imagine, and feels it's time he came out to face them. He's particularly anxious to be written up objectively and he asked me to approach you first.'

'Me?'

'But yes. You've been nominated as young journalist of the year, I understand?'

'I have?' It was news to Merril.

'Oh, dear, the wretched grapevine again! Now are you free this afternoon?'

'No, I——' A shadow fell across her desk. It was Ray. 'Yes,' she corrected. 'But I can't do it.'

The features editor had risen from her chair and was leaning forward in evident interest. I hate these open-plan offices, thought Merril, turning her back and coming face to face with Ray again.

'Do it!' he mouthed, folding his arms as if he intended to keep her there until she agreed.

'But I only interview political figures,' she said into the phone, speaking as much for Ray's benefit and that of the rest of the office. They all knew it was a blatant lie, but did Sally Hamilton?

She did. 'We saw an excellent profile of an ice hockey player recently. Wasn't that yours?' she asked.

Grudgingly Merril had to admit it. With Ray, the features editor, not to mention Damian, whose manner was ambivalent, she had no choice but to say yes.

'A car will pick you up at two p.m.'

Replacing the receiver, she felt a sigh of relief go round the office. One or two of the younger subs had picked up the atmosphere, and word quickly passed round that Merril had been singled out to interview Torrin Anthony.

'Anybody would think I'd been granted an audience with the Queen,' she grumbled as she went to fetch a cup of coffee. But secretly she was intrigued. At least it helped to take her mind off Azur for five minutes.

She had managed to get no further than the first paragraph with her article about meeting a latter-day Lawrence of Arabia, and maybe it would help to compare the two men. Similar in physique—even she had to admit that—but one blond, rugged, tough, a man of action, the other a rather languid, dark-haired actor, afraid it seemed, of even making a speech in front of a crowd of admirers without the security of a script in his hands! She couldn't imagine why he had asked specifically for her to conduct the great interview, but if he thought she was going to write the usual sycophantic rubbish he was in for a nasty shock!

The car that was sent for her arrived prompt at two o'clock. It caused a minor sensation when it whispered to a halt outside the plate glass doors of the office block where *News and Views* had the fifth floor. It wasn't every day that humble journalists were whisked to the daily grind by a Silver Shadow. It came complete with uniformed driver.

Was I right or was I right when I guessed he had a wealthy family supporting him? Merril asked herself as she sank down into the lush interior and fixed a blank expression on to her face to show how unimpressed she was. This would all go down in the notebook, but not in the admiring terms Torrin Anthony was no doubt counting on.

Feeling as if she had arrived by magic carpet, she climbed out as soon as the chauffeur stopped and came round to open the door. They had pulled up outside an imposing Regency mansion in its own grounds near the park. The passing London traffic was a discreet roar in the distance, and with plenty of mature beeches and horse-chestnuts about she could almost imagine she was in the countryside and not ten minutes by Rolls from Piccadilly Circus.

A butler stood at the top of a shallow flight of steps and she was ushered into a magnificent entrance hall—all marble domes and crystal chandeliers. This has to be a joke, she thought, looking round for a sign of the owner. A man was waiting at the top of the stairs and he came forward as the butler indicated for her to go up.

It was only as she drew level that Merril felt a vague flicker of recognition. He came to a standstill on the tread above her, looking down at her with obvious amusement.

In black denims, a matching sweat-shirt and a pair of designer running shoes, the sort that cost as much as a small stereo, she observed, he didn't look like one of the servants, but nor did he look as if he owned this pile of expensive real estate, either. He stepped in front of her as she made to go on up and she side-stepped, half turning to glance back at the butler to see if she should go on. But the stranger put out a hand. 'You don't recognise me, do you?'

She stared up into his face, wrinkling her brow as she tried without success to place him.

Clean-shaven, with a very impressive jaw, aggressive nose and hooded eyes, his hair was viciously short and looked as if it had just been cut. It formed a light blond stubble all over a rather beautifully shaped head. He could stand in for a model for one of those Greek sculptures any time, she remembered thinking, then her glance swivelled to his eyes again, a blush spreading like sudden fire up the back of her neck and into the roots of her hair.'

Everybody reminded her of Azur these days. Even now, in this ridiculous situation . . . She took a deep breath. 'Have we met?' she asked.

The man gave a soft laugh. 'Follow me.' Without further explanation he turned, and before she could object he ran two at a time up the wide staircase, pausing only briefly at the top to make sure she was following, before hurrying along the gallery to a door at the far end. 'Here, sit down. Make yourself at home.'

Merril laughed inwardly at this last remark, trying not to goggle at the palatial apartment into which he led her. He was watching her closely, too closely, making her feel clumsy. She hovered just inside the doorway.

'What about a drink—tea, coffee, or something else?'

He closed the door, coming close, making her flinch, the same look of amusement across his face with which he had greeted her. His movements were quick, decisive, as if he wasn't used to having much spare time, organising her entrance into the room, settling her into a capacious sofa beside one of the floor-length windows with that same bright glance of expectation.

'I don't believe it,' she stated flatly. Of course that brief similarity to Azur was crazy, and it was disconcerting to find herself face to face with someone who had such a strange resemblance to the man she dreamed of meeting again one day. But she had indeed met the man grinning so infuriatingly at her now. She felt like a fool. 'Without the black stage wig and eighteenth-century gear, you look quite different,' she admitted in a dazed voice.

'Isn't it amazing what a little artifice can do?' he murmured, putting his head on one side and smiling down at her. 'It frightens me sometimes how people can react so strongly to the physical appearance and miss so totally what lies underneath.'

To hide her confusion Merril scrabbled in her bag for her notebook.

'Wait.' He held up both hands. 'Let me get you a drink. What'll it be?'

'Coffee, please—black.'

While he went through another door which she had already mentally decided to describe as stage left in her article, she admitted ruefully that he had won the first round. She had been totally nonplussed, first by the mansion which he appeared to inhabit in such opulent style, and secondly by the unexpectedness of his appearance. He looked quite different from the way he'd looked the night before. Tougher, certainly not at all foppish. In fact, altogether disturbing—almost ascetic, like a monk, with that savagely short haircut and hard, clean-cut features. It suited him, of course, and he must realise how striking he looked. Beautiful, she grudgingly admitted as she scribbled a few notes, if such a word could properly describe the austere maleness of his appearance.

Feeling wrong-footed, she was just preparing to open a counter-attack with a searching question or two about the advantages of coming from such a privileged background when he appeared suddenly with the drinks, and before she got her mouth open he asked casually, 'Why do you hate actors so much? I would have thought we were a pretty harmless bunch on the whole.'

'That's probably why,' she replied, too late realising she had risen at once to the bait. 'Life's too short to spend in being harmless.'

'Ah, the intrepid war reporter. I read your piece about the uprising in——'

'I'm surprised,' she cut in. 'I wouldn't imagine world affairs were your *métier*.'

'I do emerge from the eighteenth century once in a

while,' he replied mildly, settling down next to her on the sofa in what seemed unnecessary proximity. She edged away to prevent the entire length of his leg pressing against her own.

'I think it necessary to keep in touch,' he went on. 'It's an actor's job to interpret the world, and he can hardly do that if he knows nothing of it.'

'You, obviously, know rather more than most——' Merril said, without bothering to veil her sarcasm as she glanced critically round the impressively beautiful room in which they were sitting. 'It must say something for your imagination if you can summon up a knowledge of the world from the midst of this privileged cocoon.'

'The world?'

'The one in which real people live.'

'Real people?' he queried.

'Ordinary people. Ones who have to work hard for every penny they get——'

'Oh, real people,' he broke in, nodding, as if she had mentioned some rare species.

She gave him a quick glance, imagining she detected a note of derision in his velvety voice, but his expression was appropriately blank.

'Of course,' he went on smoothly, 'it's always a great danger to jump to conclusions. Snap judgements aren't *always* accurate.'

Merril again had the uncomfortable feeling he was teasing her, but there was no flicker of amusement in the golden-brown eyes. It struck her that it was an unusual combination—dark lashes, black, in fact, with that light brown-blond hair. Perhaps they were dyed, to match the stage wig.

'How long have you lived here?' she asked, firmly opening her notebook at a clean page.

'That's a little like the question "When did you stop beating your wife?" ' he countered.

'I beg your pardon?'

'It's based on an assumption. I thought I'd warned you about snap judgements?' he remarked mildly. He was leaning back now and giving her face a close scrutiny that brought two red spots of anger to her cheeks. She bit her lip and tried to keep cool. There were always difficult ones. It was part of the job. But it needed every ounce of her training not to chip in with some cutting rejoinder. The trouble was, he reminded her uncomfortably of Azur—but it was monstrous to compare the two men. They were as unalike as wine and water. She schooled herself to wait, giving him time to go on. When he did, she was as confused as ever.

'You really don't recognise me, do you? I thought it was because you were embarrassed.'

'I didn't at first, but I do now. And why should I be embarrassed?'

He sighed and looked down at his hands. 'That was a very good article,' he said after a rather long pause.

'Thank you.' She didn't need reminding of Azur in this context. 'May we get back to you?'

He gave her an odd look. 'What would you like to know?'

'Everything.'

'That's a tall order in the time we have.' He gave a fleeting, slightly crooked smile. 'Do you expect me to put myself entirely in your hands and let you savage your way through my life just like that?' He broke off. 'I've never done one of these before. I've always avoided the press. It seems——' He hesitated, as if searching for the right word. 'It seems like the height of vanity to unload every detail about oneself and one's ambitions, and have it published to the world at large.' He shrugged and the smile flashed unexpectedly. 'That's what you want, I suppose—the bared soul. I had hoped you would guide me through it . . . gently?' he suggested, raising his eyebrows.

Does he think he can get round me to write the usual tosh by appealing to me in this way? Merril asked herself, deliberately forcing herself to resist his undoubted appeal. This false humility makes me cringe. Everybody knows actors love publicity.

Once again she felt he was amused about something, but he had the actor's knack of being able to wipe expression from his face at will. He observed her tightening lips.

'Now I've offended you by trying to appeal to your sympathy.' He rose to his feet so suddenly, she dropped her notepad, and as she bent to pick it up he said, 'This isn't working, is it? I confess I don't quite know how to handle the situation——'

Merril raised a flushed face to his. 'Oh come, Mr Anthony, just be yourself if you can.' She felt herself flounder like a complete beginner, then, unforgivably, heard herself ask, 'Are you trying to say I'm no good at my job?'

'You're obviously very good at your job—such as it is,' he added, just as she was beginning to feel a curl of satisfaction that he should recognise the fact. 'But I don't think much of the press at the best of times. And your interviewing technique leaves something to be desired,' he added, wounding her pride even further. 'You're supposed to put me at my ease, aren't you? Instead I feel anything I say will be taken down and used in evidence against me. I particularly wanted to avoid the sort of sparring game that characterises so much of one's dealings with the media—as if they're all the time trying to discover some skeleton in the cupboard. There are none in mine and I resent being made to feel there are.'

'You haven't given me a chance!' she flared. 'You're the one who asked to be interviewed, though why the hell you asked for me I shall never know. Especially after last night.'

'Yes, that was a mistake,' he agreed, 'but I was willing to make allowances for last night. It was an odd situation for both of us, I fancy. All those people!' He smiled disarmingly and ran a hand over the cropped hair. 'I asked for you,' he went on, 'because, among other reasons, I thought you could be fairly objective.'

His criticism of her anything but objective behaviour stung Merril's professional pride. 'I *can* be objective, as I'm sure you'll find,' she retorted. 'So let's begin . . . How does it feel to be flavour of the month, Mr Anthony?' she asked, pencil poised.

'Wonderful. What do you expect me to say? Everyone wants to be liked, don't they?' He sat down in the chair opposite.

'You more than most, perhaps?'

'Do you think so?' His eyes pierced hers, bright as tiger stone.

'I'm supposed to be asking the questions.'

'Quite right. Fire away.' His lips curved slightly.

'Is this your father's house?'

'What?' He looked round at the chandeliered room as if suddenly surprised to find himself sitting in the midst of such opulence. 'No, not exactly.'

'What's that supposed to mean?' demanded Merril.

'It means it's not my father's house. Look,' he said hurriedly, 'aren't you supposed to ask me about what parts I've played, what parts I hope to play, what I think about theatre in general, stardom, integrity, my favourite directors, even what my first part was——?'

'What was it?'

'Third shepherd in a school Nativity play.'

She had a mental picture of the roguish shepherd

he would make, a picture which was quickly stifled.

'You'd like it to stay at that level, wouldn't you? Hoping I'll write the usual sort of drivel, praising you to the skies?' She leaned back against the soft cushions. 'That's it, isn't it?' She watched him. His expression gave nothing away. 'You want a paean to the glory of Torrin Anthony, celebrated genius of the stage, famous——' She was about to say stud but thought better of it. There was something dangerous in his stillness. She leaned forward. 'Let's get one thing straight, Mr Anthony, you won't get that from me. I'm not some stupid gossip columnist, waiting to jump on the latest band-wagon, helping turn the latest name into a star for the dubious privilege of being first on the gravy train. I write as I find, and my only aim is the truth.'

'Fighting talk,' he added drily.

Merril started to put her notepad back in her shoulder-bag and, undeterred, went on, 'I saw the way you pretended to be tongue-tied at that first-night party when they asked you for a speech. I mean, really! You might fool most people, but I'm not so gullible. As if an actor with your experience would have qualms about getting up in front of a few friends——' She was surprised he hadn't tried to interrupt her. 'It's obvious I can't do this assignment. I didn't want to do it in the first place. And I'm certainly not going to give you the puff you want. I'll hand you over to someone else.' She rose to her feet and stood uncertainly when he still didn't try to stop her. 'It's the sort of job I hate. Even this house! I mean, look at it! It's exactly the sort of place someone obsessed by stardom like you would choose. It's nothing but a theatrical backdrop, designed to impress. Well, it doesn't impress me and you've made a bad mistake if you think otherwise. I can't imagine why you thought I'd write the sort of article you want.' She made a move towards the door. 'We may as well stop now.'

'Sit down.'

'What?' She was pulled up short by the quiet coldness of his tone.

'You heard.'

She gazed at him in stupefaction, then a smile broke over her face. 'What's happened to the charm now? Is this the real Torrin Anthony? The one lurking beneath the façade?'

'Shut up, will you?'

She laughed in his face. 'The veneer is quite thin, after all!'

His tone was very even. 'You'd like me to lose my temper, wouldn't you? You're like the rest of your kind—desperate to get your teeth into any little failing. I said, sit down.'

'I heard you.' Merril remained standing and took out her notebook with insolent deliberation, but before she could open it he moved quickly across the intervening space and took it out of her hands, sending it flying across the coffee-table where it slithered over the Italian marble and fell on to the carpet on the other side.

Merril looked at it in astonishment. Before she could register a protest, he pushed her down on to the sofa and stood glowering down at her. She was surgingly conscious of his physical power. He had a contained feline presence, like a wildcat waiting to pounce. Their glances meshed, her own gripped despite her wishes by the intensity of his.

'I don't often lose my temper, but you really push your luck, lady. Is this show of bad manners part of the objective journalism you're so proud of?' His eyes narrowed to gold slits. 'What's really eating you? Or does honesty stop when it comes to turning it on yourself?'

'I don't know what you mean!' She tried to struggle to her feet.

'Sit still. I haven't finished——'

'Don't you dare touch me!'

'Very Victorian!' he mocked as she flinched away from the hand he placed on her shoulder to keep her in her place. His grip tightened. 'Well? Was it a waste of time asking you here? Did I overestimate you? Are you as trivial and bigoted as the usual run of muck-rakers that litter your profession?'

'How dare you?'

'I haven't said anything yet,' he growled. 'Tell me,' he went on in mock conversational tones, 'what do you imagine gives you the right to throw insults without a comeback? Sit still!' He suddenly slid down beside her so that she was effectively wedged against the end of the sofa. 'You came here to do a job and you're going to do it, and if you imagine I'm going to let you walk out of here with all your prejudices intact, you couldn't be more wrong.'

'Prejudices?' she echoed.

'That's what I said. This ridiculous prejudice about actors, for instance.'

'No worse than yours about journalists!' Merril spat back.

'We're not all charlatans,' he went on as if she hadn't spoken. 'Some of us take the job seriously. Or is it just me you dislike, for some reason?' He cocked an eyebrow. 'I don't know the answer to that one. I doubt whether you do either. You have such a warped view, I wonder what's behind it?'

'Warped? How dare you?'

'You should be pleased I'm giving you some copy and not throwing you out on your ear as you deserve. You can write it all up for your filthy paper.'

'You bet I shall! It'll open a few eyes! People'll like nothing better than to discover the truth about the great Torrin Anthony, Mr Wonderful himself, with a filthy rotten side to his oh, so charming personality!'

'You'd love to be the one to put the boot in, wouldn't you? Nothing would give you greater pleasure than to run against the crowd if you could . . . anything to be different. You accused me of hypocrisy, but I should say that's precisely the name of your own game. Fearless investigative reporter. Quake, all ye hypocrites and thieves, Miss Park's tongue-lashing is a thing to be feared.' He broke off, his expression puzzled rather than angry.

'Stop being so paranoid, Mr Anthony. You don't expect every woman to throw herself at your feet, do you? You can't win them all. You leave me stone cold. It must be a new experience——'

'Cold? Now we are on ground I know about,' he murmured suggestively. Somehow the arm that was resting on the sofa behind her back slowly began to draw her against him, and even as she struggled to get to her feet she felt a betraying slackness in her limbs, a yielding to the undoubted physical attraction she had felt from the first. To her surprise, he didn't try to kiss her. Instead he held her against him so she could hear his heart beating with her own.

'Yes,' he said after a moment or two as he felt her anger begin to evaporate, 'that's better. That's much better. Now, shall we start from the beginning?' He held her face between two hands and Merril began to tremble as he gazed into her eyes.

CHAPTER THREE

'DON'T try it on,' she managed to whisper. 'You tried this technique on me in your dressing-room last night and it didn't work then either——'

'Technique? You mean when I kissed your sweet little hands? You thought it was some sort of try-on?' His voice was husky. 'I couldn't believe my eyes when I saw you, Merril. Surely you could see that? I wanted to make sure you were real.'

'Stop it, please! I'm——'

'Yes?' The pressure of his fingers on either side of her jaw was sending shivers of pure pleasure over her. She remembered Azur, the magic of his touch, and tried to pull away.

'If you think this means I'm going to go back on what I said, you're mistaken,' she told him through trembling lips. 'You're simply confirming my first impression of you.' She tried to turn her head to lessen the effect of those eyes blazing over her face, but he gently turned her face up to his again.

'First impressions? Tell me your first impressions, Merril.'

'Of you?' Her lip curled.

His manner told her he wasn't going to let her escape. All right, she thought before she began, you asked for it!'

She furrowed her brow as if making an effort to recall the previous night, as if it wasn't printed indelibly on her mind. 'It looked to me,' she began, 'as if you were enjoying all that flattery——'

'When?' he interrupted, frowning.

'Last night, of course.'

'Oh . . .' He gave her an odd look. 'Go on.'

'You looked delighted with it.' She paused. 'Crazy for it. It was sickening to see all those stupid women with their vulgar clothes and artificial smiles, cooing and simpering all over you! Especially when it was so obvious why they were doing it!'

'And why was that—in your unbiased view?' he asked quietly.

She paused, blushed, and, catching sight of something dangerous in his eyes, corrected the reply she was about to make. No point in adding to the size of his ego—he already knew he had sex appeal! 'They simply wanted to be seen with somebody famous,' she hedged. '*You* happened to fit the bill.'

'I'm not famous. Well, I wasn't last night when the curtain rose. This morning things seem to be somewhat different.' A pile of newspapers with his name splashed all over them were mute testimony to what he was saying.

'I don't blame you for lapping it all up,' Merril went on, her voice dripping sympathy. 'It's not everyone who has your luck. Instant stardom! Wonderful for your poor ego. Enjoy it while you can. Why not?' She gave a little shrug as if to say, if that's what you want, more fool you. But the patronising note wasn't lost on him.

'You see me, then, as some kind of gadfly?' he asked quietly. 'Heir to a brief summer of fame and a long winter of obscurity?'

She smiled faintly. 'Quite.'

He gave her a long, regarding look, the honey-coloured eyes ambivalent, the long, full line of his mobile mouth giving nothing away.

'Merril,' he spoke her name like a caress, making her shiver with unbidden memory, but before she had time to place it he went on, 'you must understand one thing about me—nothing I do is done lightly. I don't dedicate myself to an ephemeral art because I have a gadfly approach. Nothing could be further from the truth. I take my work seriously. Fame means little to me. What I do, I do to last, through summer, through winter. It's the same with everything I do. That's how I am.'

His eyes crinkled. 'There's also something to be said for a night of ecstasy, a dawn of sheer delight——' He smiled directly into her eyes as if to share a special secret, but she tore her glance away, angry at the turmoil of her own emotions and shown up by his disarming honesty. If she'd hoped she could taunt him into betraying an unworthy side of himself, she had miscalculated again. Now he gave the impression that he knew a lot more than she did, and it made her seethe with humiliation.

'You're treating me as if I'm some clumsy, inexperienced schoolgirl,' she muttered, reddening. She tried to move away, only managing to wedge herself even more tightly against the end of the sofa. 'I don't have to stand for this, Mr Anthony. I know when I'm having the wool pulled over my eyes. I told you I wouldn't fall for it. As far as I'm concerned, our interview is over. You've given me all the material I need. I'll write it up—at your request,' she added meaningfully, 'but I'm afraid you won't like the result.'

'I won't? Be careful, Merril, or it'll be "gadfly bites back".'

'Are you threatening me?' she flared.

'Oh, that's a good one! "Star threatens girl reporter"—but is it spicy enough? What about "Star threatens girl reporter in sex interview scandal"? And are you sure you can't work in a wife-swap vicar or two as well?'

'I work for a quality paper, Mr Anthony, as I know

you've already taken the trouble to discover. *And*,' she added as an afterthought, 'I wasn't aware that *sex* came into this so-called interview. Your imagination's running away with you. Now if you don't mind, I can't sit here——'

'Hold it!' He placed a finger on her lips before she could avert her head, and then his other hand came round the back of her head, and she could feel his fingers sliding through the tresses of her hair. 'I'd like to rectify things, just to make your account more authentic.'

'What?' Before she could fathom what he meant, he brought her face up to his and placed a kiss gently and briefly on her lips. Merril gave a little gasp, told herself to pull away, but too late felt her lips respond. Her chin tilted of its own accord, lifting to feel his touch again Her eyes closed as she saw his mouth come down on hers. This time his kiss was deep; it was a moment out of time. She couldn't fight it, was swept helplessly along in a torrent of unexpected emotion. When they finally drew apart they were both breathless. Merril felt dazed by images of Azur; she could almost hear the cicadas singing.

Suddenly his image was so powerful, the loss of that brief paradise such pain, that a cry was wrenched from her throat and she flailed out wildly at the face in front of her, snaking out of her place so quickly that he didn't have time to stop her.

'Get away from me!' she snarled, all the pain at having betrayed a memory filling her voice with hate.

Torrin Anthony's face paled, but he sprang after her, striding over the coffee-table and gripping her by both wrists before she could reach the door. 'What's the matter?' His voice was hoarse. 'What have I done?'

'I knew my first impression was right!' she shouted. 'You can't bear anybody not to fall under your spell. You're like a snake charmer! But you can't charm me! I'm not going to fall for you—no way! Not me!' Her heart filled with self-disgust at how nearly she had allowed herself to be seduced. After a kiss like that, the consequences would be inevitable. No woman would be able to resist his practised skill—there would be heartbreak as he first used, then discarded her. She knew exactly what he was underneath the charming mask.

Now he was trying to smooth-talk his way out of the situation. 'I wouldn't offend you for the world, Merril.' He tried to take her hand, but she dashed it away. 'But why are you reacting like this? Isn't it strange after——'

'Strange?' she stormed. 'To someone with your giant ego, anyone who doesn't throw themselves all over you must seem strange!'

'Not at all. I can't be everyone's type. I don't care about all that, anyway,' he said hurriedly. 'What's it got to do with us?'

'Us?' she echoed.

'Yes, us, Merril, here and now. You wanted me to kiss you. And I wanted to kiss you very much indeed——'

'I don't go around letting strangers kiss me like that——' she broke in.

'No?' He raised his eyebrows.

'*No!*' she shouted defiantly, too defiantly, because she knew, though he couldn't, that it wasn't true. Azur's ruffianly blond image taunted her again.

'I told you, I don't do anything lightly, Merril. I want to make love to you——' he gave her a one-sided smile '—though I can see it's not the moment to tell you this.' He went on, 'I wanted to make love to you from the first moment I saw you. My theory, for what it's worth, is if love's the real thing, it's there from the moment of meeting. Maybe I'm an old-fashioned romantic, but that's how it's got to be with me.'

'You'd get on well with my flatmate,' she muttered, furious to find herself listening to his smooth tongue even now. 'Eyes across a crowded room?' she mocked.

'I don't believe in the sort of love that springs from friendship. It must always lack passion. For me, love has to be a passionate affair, a conflagration, an instant meeting of souls. I know I would never want us to be mere friends.'

'Thank you,' she said stiffly, wondering whether to feel flattered or insulted.

'Try to understand what I'm saying,' he went on. 'I've lived a life dedicated to work. Surely if you've noticed anything about me, you'll have noticed that? It means I haven't planned for love. I don't want it.' His face was harsh. 'But if I turn away from this——' he spread his hands '—I feel I shall be turning my back on something powerful and——' His voice vibrated with emotion. 'Understand . . . I don't find any of this easy. I'm not . . . it's not my style. Merril, I don't make love to every woman I meet.'

There were so many hesitations in his speech, he sounded suspiciously like a lovesick schoolboy, stammering out his feelings. His expression tugged at Merril's heart and she took a pace towards him, something powerful driving her forward until she remembered who he was and what he was.

It sent her stepping hurriedly back.

'Well acted,' she remarked in a voice like ice, clapping her hands ironically. 'Bravo, Mr Anthony! You nearly convinced me you meant it. Are those lines from your next role?'

For a moment there was silence. Torrin Anthony stared at her, his face wiped of expression. She felt she could see him decide which role to adopt next as the last one had been such a signal failure, but with a small lift and fall of his right hand he turned away to one of the windows. Although she couldn't observe his face, she could see the movement of the broad shoulders as if they were trying to move a huge block, like the weight of some terrible emotion on them.

He can even act with his back to the audience, she noted disparagingly, her mind like ice while her emotions raged red-hot at the memory of his touch. It made things easier if she fixed her mind on Azur.

But his silence drew an unexpected compulsion to explain before she left. 'I admit you're attractive, exactly the sort of figure most women go for,' she said, surprised at the sound of her voice: small, cold, definite. 'But you see, the thing is, I'm more impressed by men of action, not the actor type, and besides, I'm already committed to someone.'

He jerked round. 'Who?'

'No one you could possibly know.'

'That theatre critic chap? Surely not?' He came towards her, looking bewildered.

Merril shook her head.

He gave a smile that didn't reach his eyes. 'Tell me about him.'

'I can't.'

'Why not?'

'It's simply too painful—hopeless,' she admitted, wondering why her voice had dropped to a whisper.

In a few strides he was right across the room. 'I do apologise for what I did just now—it was too soon. Sit down, Merril. Let's talk—as friends.'

'I thought you said we——'

'Forget what I said. Tell me,' he took her by the hand and led her to the sofa, this time sitting at a reasonable distance from her, 'who is this man? Why is it painful? Is he married?'

'It's a long story. It's——' She closed her eyes.

'No—I must leave.'

'Please!' He took her by the hand.

'He's the sort of man I've always dreamed of . . .' Then, not daring to look at him, she found herself telling him about her brief encounter, omitting Azur's name because it was too private, but telling him about the circumstances in which they met, of his bravery, his toughness, his humour, his devastating good looks, and his masterful handling of the dangerous situation they had been in and, finally, how like her own father he was.

'Your father?' he prompted, shaking himself out of a protracted silence.

'In his time he was a famous war correspondent. The old-timers in Fleet Street still talk about him. He was killed on an assignment in the Far East when I was ten.'

'I see.' He looked thoughtful. 'That's a very sensitive age.'

'No one will really live up to him,' she said with conviction.

'Merril,' his voice was gentle, 'don't you realise that this brief encounter of yours with this man is mixed up with feelings about your father? It's mainly fantasy. You're still mourning your father's death. It can happen when feelings are repressed for some reason. This Azur seems to have accidentally triggered off forgotten feelings of grief. In real life he's probably just an ordinary fellow . . . with a wife and children,' he added, as an afterthought.

'No!' Merril shook her head vehemently. 'You don't understand. He was extraordinary. And I'm sure he'd have told me if he'd been married. You see, we spent a night together——' She broke off. It was too painful. She felt a knot of tears lodged inside her skull. 'He was like Dad, living a life of danger a man like you could never begin to understand.'

His manner became abrupt. 'It's escapism, an adolescent fantasy. You know nothing about the man.'

'And I suppose I never shall,' she remarked, biting her lip. 'I'm resigned to the fact we shall never meet again.'

'Very romantic! And having accepted that, you feel nice and safe dreaming your life away for someone who can never erupt into reality.' Torrin Anthony's tone was unaccountably savage.

'But I long to meet him again,' she told him, turning astonished blue eyes to his.

'Could you take the shock of discovering he's really quite ordinary?'

'But he's not! I know he's not! He's special and wonderful and not at all ordinary!'

'Then why don't you see him?' he challenged.

'How can I?' she exclaimed. 'I do have a job. I can't just go back when I feel like it.'

'It would lay a few ghosts if you did.' He took hold of her by the shoulders, a bemused expression on his face. 'I'd like to shake some sense into you——' he said half to himself. 'But I've got a better idea.' Dragging her with him, he picked up her notebook from the floor, handing it back to her with a cryptic, 'Wait here a minute.'

Puzzled, Merril put her book away while he went into the next room. When he returned he wore a guarded look. 'Come along.'

He strode over and took her by the arm without looking at her, but when he started to lead her towards the door she wrenched herself away. 'Wait a minute——'

He gripped her more strongly by the upper arm so that she was forced towards the door. 'Don't make a scene,' he warned. 'The servants don't speak English and it would only worry them.'

'Why should *I* care?' she exclaimed, giving him a startled glance. She began to struggle as he propelled her towards the stairs.

'I'm stronger than you, so don't waste your energy.'

'You damned bully, Torrin Anthony! Is this the real you at last?'

'You wouldn't recognise the real me if you were handed a diagram with arrows.'

Before she could protest further he began to hustle her down the staircase to the hall. The butler appeared and discreetly opened the door, and Merril found herself being pushed down the steps towards a waiting car. It wasn't the Rolls that had brought her to the house, but a large, sleek black Jaguar with smoked glass windows. She half expected a couple of gangsters to be sitting inside, but the lush leather interior was empty.

'Where are we going?' she protested even as the door closed and Torrin settled in beside her. The car swept powerfully down the drive towards the road through the park before he answered.

'If you haven't yet realised it, Miss Merril Park, you're being kidnapped. Now lie back and enjoy it,' he answered brutally.

CHAPTER FOUR

AT FIRST she thought he was joking. 'Let me out, will you?' Her lips compressed in an irritable line.

'Out? Oh, no. I'm not letting you out.'

'Mr Anthony, this has gone on long enough. If we get on to the M25,' Merril added, peering out of the window, 'I'm going to have the devil of a job getting back to Fleet Street.'

'You're not going back to Fleet Street. Not today, anyway.'

'Don't be ridiculous!'

'I gather from Doyle, your boss, you've got five days off work. Well,' he smiled grimly, 'that should be five days before anybody realises you're missing.'

'Look here, stop being so ridiculous and let me out, will you?' She glanced wildly from his face—grim, to the back of the driver's head—unheeding, with the glass partition between them.

'I wouldn't bother,' Torrin told her, observing the direction of her glance. 'As I've already told you, none of the servants speak English, not enough for your no doubt intricate explanations, anyway. So you may as well just settle down and enjoy it.'

'Enjoy?' She gaped. 'Enjoy being made a fool of? Stop this pretence and set me down!'

'And not even a please,' he murmured, unperturbed by her angry face. He gave a disarming smile that only served to antagonise her more and said, 'I've already told you, it's no pretence, so settle down.'

'I won't! I'll——' Merril glanced out to the swiftly moving stream of traffic through which the Jaguar

71

was nosing with impressive assurance. Soon they would be on the throughway out of central London, and then what?

Torrin crystallised her predicament when he pointed out that if she tried anything silly it would be doomed to failure. 'You wouldn't risk physical injury by trying to throw yourself from a moving car, would you?'

'I may be risking physical injury by submitting to this so-called kidnapping!' she retorted.

'No,' he replied softly, 'never that. Not with me. You know I would never hurt you.'

The fact that he *could* hurt her, that he could do anything at all to her when they got to their destination, sank in with horrid suddenness as the car continued to bear them rapidly out of central London. Soon they were being driven through the endless miles of northern suburbs, through Hampstead and out past the Heath, far from any possibility of help. She expected the car to draw to a halt soon in some leafy driveway, but it swept onwards until she lost any sense of where they were heading.

Having failed to seize any opportunity to escape, she had a bitter smile on her face when she announced in a small voice, 'All right, Mr Anthony, you win for now. But,' she paused, lifting her chin with an unmistakable flicker of triumph as she added, 'this won't look good in the papers.'

'Papers? What papers?' he asked mildly.

'*My* paper, for one,' she derided, gaining strength from the idea, 'I'm going to go to town on you!'

'It'll look very good,' he agreed. 'When everyone realises we've spent five days together in my secret love-nest, they'll put two and two together and make six as usual. And when you come to write up a bitchy article afterwards, they'll make some interesting computations then, too.'

'What do you mean?' she asked suspiciously.

'Obvious, isn't it? We all know I'm London's latest "heart-throb",' he explained, quoting a phrase used in one of the morning papers, 'and when you start bitching after our weekend of love they'll simply assume it's the anger of a woman spurned. Hell hath no fury, and so forth. I wouldn't give twopence for your chances against the hacks of the gutter Press. They'll have a field day. You'll be able to make a tidy killing. Intimate details and all that. "My night of passion, by blonde newshound." They'll probably ask you to pose topless, too—it's just the sort of story the press love.' He chuckled, and Merril flinched as his eyes raked appraisingly over her body, patently enjoying the idea of her half undressed before a posse of grinning press photographers.

'You wouldn't dare——'

'I don't have to do a thing,' he pointed out, 'so daring doesn't come into it.'

'But I'd lose all credibility——' Her mouth worked, though no words would come out.

'You certainly would.'

'I couldn't carry on as a political correspondent with that sort of publicity——'

'You couldn't.'

'But that's blackmail!' Merril's fists bunched helplessly. 'You bastard!' she croaked after a pause. 'I believe you've deliberately planned this in order to compromise me!'

Torrin ran a finger down the side of her cheek. 'No, I didn't plan it. It was a sudden impulse. But it's certainly working out well, isn't it?'

'For you, yes!' she snarled, nearly beside herself with impotent rage. 'I'll never forgive you for this! As soon as I get near a phone I'm going to ring—I'm going to ring——' She stopped.

'Yes?'

She couldn't ring Ray. That would be to betray her own incompetence to the very man she needed to impress if work of the sort she wanted was still to come her way. And she couldn't tell Damian, either. He would never believe she'd walked into a situation like this with her eyes wide open. He would think it an excuse because she'd been unable to resist the promise of a brief fling with the man of the moment. Then she concealed a smile. There was Annie. Good old Annie. She would get her help, ask her to call in the police if necessary. Make a big thing of it—missing war correspondent, Annie's frantic appeals to the kidnappers—she could see it all on the six o'clock news. Kidnapping was a serious offence. If she could only prove she had been brought away against her will, then even Torrin Anthony's charm wouldn't get him out of that!

She gazed out of the window at the fields unfolding rapidly from the horizon like a long strip of coloured cloth. It was no good making a scene now because there was no one to witness it, but later, when the driver opened the door, she would make a dash for it. Pity he didn't speak English, but even if he couldn't tell what she was saying, he would be able to discern the panic in her face, her complete unwillingness to go with the man who was his master.

Settling back with her blonde head resting against the wine-coloured leather cushions, Merril let her eyes close. Best if her captor thought she was giving in to his power mania, then she could take him by surprise.

Mile after mile sped by, and it was late afternoon when the car swung off the M11 and began a circuitous journey down a country road. In a few minutes it bumped over a cattle grid and whispered down a track through a meadow full of celandines, coming at last to a sighing halt in a grove of oaks.

Torrin had already opened the door as the car slowed, and he pushed Merril out ahead of him, tapping on the driver's window as he stepped forward. Before she could gather her wits, the car continued its smooth arc and in a second it was disappearing back along the road they had just travelled.

'Wait! Come back!' Arms waving, she stumbled after it, her plan in ruins as her last chance of help dwindled into the distance. The silence after it had gone was profound.

Then all the violence of her emotions came tumbling forth in a stream of oaths. She wanted to beat her fists into Torrin Anthony's grinning face, but she knew if she dared lay a finger on him retribution, despite his words, would be inevitable. She was helpless, and he knew it. She would have given anything to wipe that insufferable smugness off his face. But there was nothing she could do. Her body sagged.

'All right,' he said. 'So now you understand anger isn't going to get you anywhere, shall we walk?'

'Walk?' Merril shrugged weakly, the fight going out of her.

He slipped an arm in hers. 'Not far. I can see you're tired.'

'I am not tired,' she muttered defiantly, even now determined not to concede the smallest thing to him, but she let him lead her across the grove towards a narrow path that led into the bushes. Somewhere behind the thick bank of pollards was a faint sound of rushing water. As they walked down the path it got louder, and then Merril saw a narrow plank bridge over a stream and ahead of them a house.

It was a millhouse, complete with wooden waterwheel mirrored in the still green depths of a pool, and the sight was so unexpectedly picturesque that Merril stopped with a small gasp. Its roof swept low on the garden side, starred by the tiny blossoms of an early flowering clematis, making it shimmer like a precious jewel in a rich setting, and it was all so exactly what a secret love-nest should be that she felt a premonition of dismay that for her it would be anything but.

Ignoring her reaction, Torrin marched on ahead, a key already gleaming in his hand. As he unlocked the door, he gave an apologetic smile. 'Although there are all mod cons, I'm afraid there's no phone. The nearest village is miles away. It suits me,' he added, 'when I need to get away from it all.'

'Why don't you have to be at the theatre tonight?' Merril asked suspiciously as she followed him into the house.

He moved on ahead over a polished parquet floor, throwing the key down on a carved table before turning, saying curtly, 'Oh, but I do. I shall make sure you're settled before I leave. And don't worry,' he went on, 'I shall be back as soon as I can.'

'You can't do this, Torrin!' It was the first time she had pronounced his name with anything but sarcasm, and she could tell he noticed.

His words, spoken lightly, confirmed it. 'Soon you'll be pleading with me,' he remarked. He regarded her in silence for a moment before adding, 'Well, maybe not just yet.'

'Not ever,' she vowed as he turned and went into another room. She gazed round, automatically taking in the lush furnishings, everything old and well worn but lovingly cared for, a scent of lavender wax on the air, fresh flowers in a large pot by one of the windows, logs already arranged in the open hearth. It would be cosy here in winter, and now, in early summer, it had a beguiling serenity. There was a promise of rain scenting the air as a window was opened in a distant room and birdsong flooded in, tugging at her heart. She went to sit on a wooden settle, but Torrin came back almost straight away.

'It'll be a quick meal, as I have to get back, but while we're waiting for it you may as well come up and see your room. Do you like turquoise?'

'It's a matter of indifference to me what colour it is,' she replied coldly.

'Black would suit your mood better, but I'm afraid the décor doesn't run to that.' He led the way up an open-tread staircase to a corridor with doors opening off both sides. Everything was deceptively spacious and gave the impression that no expense had been spared, even though there was restraint in the furnishings with nothing done to excess. Her room, as he insisted on calling it, was fresh and pretty with touches of white at the windows and a turquoise and white bedspread. There would have been ample cupboard space if she had brought any luggage with her, and there was an adequate bookshelf for a short stay, a well-lit dressing-table and a white quartz clock-radio on the bedside table. It was, she noted with a flicker of anxiety, a double bed.

Pretending she hadn't noticed this, she was relieved when Torrin mentioned that his own room was further down the corridor, with the bathroom, shower and 'all that sort of thing' in between.

When he went downstairs again to check on the promised meal, Merril did some exploration of her own and discovered that 'all that sort of thing' included a jacuzzi and a sunbed. I never realised acting was so well paid, she thought ironically. Then she remembered the palatial London house in the park. Torrin Anthony had obviously never had to grub a living for himself as most people had. It made his talk of dedication seem more like hypocrisy than

ever. When she went back downstairs an enticing
aroma of home cooking filled the kitchen, and she
disguised her appreciation under a determined show
of indifference. Torrin was peering into a large red
cooking pot, prodding at something inside it as if
unsure whether it was ready or not. 'What do you
think?' he asked as she came in.

'Don't ask me,' she replied stubbornly. 'You're in
charge.'

'But you're going to eat it, so you——'

'Am I?' she interrupted. 'You can't make me.'

'Suit yourself.' He gave a cold smile. 'But I'm
certainly going to have some. I haven't prepared it for
nothing.'

'You?' Merril retorted scathingly.

'Sorry I don't come up to the standards of your
macho lover,' he remarked. 'I admit I quite enjoy
cooking. I suppose that loses me several hundred
Brownie points on your scale. Of course,' he added in
a deliberately provoking tone, 'all the best chefs are
men.'

Ignoring her refusal to eat with him, he placed two
settings side by side at a large scrubbed table. With a
couple of red and white gingham napkins completing
the scene, Merril couldn't help admitting it looked
very homely—not at all the cosy domestic scene she
would have envisaged after the elegant formality of
the town house.

By now she was beginning to realise that she
hadn't eaten properly all day. Breakfast was always
non-existent, and she had been so annoyed by all the
fuss at the office when it was known who she was
going to interview that she had avoided the canteen
and made do with a cup of coffee and a sandwich at
her desk instead. But, hungry or not, she wasn't in a
mood to give way. Let him learn how determined she
could be when the chips were down, she thought,

and he would soon see he would have to admit defeat and let her go.

With obvious relish Torrin started on his own meal. 'It's very good . . .' he observed after a few silent moments, 'though I say it myself. Are you sure you won't change your mind?'

'Absolutely,' she affirmed, beginning to regret her obstinacy.

'Tell me, Merril,' he said after a few more moments of unfriendly silence, 'what do you hope to gain by refusing to eat with me? It's not spoiling my enjoyment. Later on I'm sure you'll wish you hadn't been so uncompromising.'

'Go to hell,' she muttered.

'Not to hell,' he remarked, rising, as there came the sound of a car horn outside, 'to heaven, or, more precisely, the boards of a West End theatre.' His smile dazzled her for a moment. He's really happy at the prospect, she thought with a surge of emotion. So much for stage fright! It was almost contagious, his relish at the thought of being on-stage. Just in time she prevented herself from smiling back.

'I hope you break a leg,' she taunted as he reached the door.

'Thank you. Good to know you're familiar with theatrical tradition.'

Too late Merril remembered this was a piece of theatre lore, like not whistling backstage or not wearing green. 'I meant it,' she scowled. 'Break both legs, and your neck as well!'

'But then I won't be able to come back and rescue you and you might remain here for ever, like the princess in the fairy story.'

'I don't know that one,' she said stiffly, turning her back. His words started up all kinds of fears in her again and, when the door closed behind him, she ran to one of the windows, half hoping it was some sort of trick and that he would return to whisk her back to town. But he crossed to the wooden footbridge without a backward glance and in a minute he was gone.

There was a strange sense of anticlimax after he had left, and she roamed listlessly about the house for a while, idly poking into the other rooms, standing agape for a minute or two at the long room that ran along the top of the house on the third floor. It was evidently Torrin Anthony's own private gym. Apart from some slick-looking weight-training equipment it was almost empty, a mirror running all the way down one side, giving it the appearance of an aerobics studio. Merril could imagine him, preening that perfect body in the mirror every morning as he worked his muscles in a rigorous work-out. Dedication, she scoffed—yes, dedication to himself and his own ego. She went back downstairs and flicked on the television. There must be a way of contacting the outside world, she pondered. Everything aside, Annie would be worried that she hadn't turned up at the flat by now.

She returned to the kitchen, gobbling down some of the supper she had already spurned straight out of the pot, hoping Torrin wouldn't notice it had gone down so much, then she went up to the turquoise room and lay down on the bed. He would be partying till the early hours, no doubt, so there wasn't much point in waiting up. She would watch the ten o'clock news, then turn in. It was horrible being so isolated. Night had already fallen and the trees on the other side of the stream seemed to press threateningly around the millhouse, reminding her of scenes from a horror movie. For a moment she gave way to tears, chiding herself, even as they flowed down her cheeks, for such patent self-pity. Then she started to think of Azur and, though her tears of pain and loss increased, somehow the image of a harsh-featured man with a stubble of a haircut and a smile like the sun breaking forth came to block out

Azur's blond good looks so that even that pleasant
wallowing in what-might-have-been was spoiled.

The bed felt like ice as she slipped between the
sheets. She had no night things and hadn't wanted to
sleep in her underwear. After rinsing out her panties
and tights she had left them on the heated towel rail to
dry. Too bad if Torrin didn't like lace panties draped all
over his bathroom. Contrary to what she expected,
sleep didn't come quickly. There were too many
strange sounds, and even though she locked the door
she felt uneasy. What Torrin's aim was in bringing her
to this remote place she couldn't guess. She had been
too proud to ask and so far he hadn't tried to explain,
beyond that terse comment at the interview that he
wasn't going to let her go away with her prejudices
intact.

When sleep did at last claim her, she slept only
fitfully, waking every so often to wonder where she
was and, remembering, drifting off again.

'Merril?' The soft voice intruding in her dreams was
familiar and she reached out, whispering, 'Azur?'
before coming fully awake. A wedge of light came in
through the door of the room. Against it she could see
the bulky outline of a man. Then she came fully awake
and sat up. Not until she felt a draught fingering over
her skin did she realise she was nude, and by then it
was too late to stop Torrin's lazy scrutiny of her naked
neck and breasts. Thankful that she couldn't see his
expression, she groped for the duvet, shuddering when
she felt him reach out and tug it from out of her fingers.

'Don't. You look so beautiful . . .' he murmured
huskily, watching the colour bloom over her skin. He
held on to one edge of the duvet, and Merril was
burningly conscious of the touch of his fingers against
her breast before she managed to pull it up. She lay
back against the pillows, surprised at the gentleness in
his voice, then shivering when she understood what

that seductive tone might portend.

'What time is it?' she asked, striving to maintain a tone of normality against the racing of her emotions.

'Just after midnight,' he told her without looking at his watch.

It was earlier than she'd thought. She hadn't been asleep as long as she'd imagined. And he was back far sooner than she had ever expected. He must have driven, or been driven, back from out of the West End like a demon, leaving as soon as the curtain came down. She felt the bed subside slightly as he sat down on the edge.

'I didn't expect you to be in bed yet. I thought we might talk.'

'What is there to say?' The sharp antagonism that had characterised her on Torrin's departure had been leavened by sleep. She could only stare hazily up at him, waiting to see what he would do next, her defences lowered but not entirely down. Recognising this, he took one of her hands in his. 'Perhaps you'd rather wait till morning? I'm a night person. I forget other people don't necessarily work by the same clock.'

'What is there to say?' she repeated, becoming frighteningly aware of what the steady pressure of his hand on her own was doing to her, and aware as he must be that she was totally naked under the protection of the single covering.

'I've brought you some things to wear,' he told her, sidetracking her question and indicating a bag standing in the doorway. Merril recognised it as one of her own.

'How did you——?' She frowned. Suddenly nothing made sense. 'Where did you get that from?' She leaned forward.

'Your friend Annie very willingly brought it round to the stage door during the performance.'

'Annie? She wouldn't——' Looking at him, she knew he was telling the truth. 'What did you tell her?' she

demanded, flushing even before he spoke at what
Annie would inevitably conclude from her absence.

'I told her you were spending the weekend with
me—doing an in-depth interview,' Torrin said softly.
'Isn't that what you will be doing?'

'I will?'

'You don't imagine I brought you here for a holiday,
do you?'

'I don't know why you brought me here, Torrin,' she
muttered, turning her head to hide the surge of
disappointment that inexplicably swept over her. It was
humiliating to admit to a desire for him after all she had
said, and she didn't want to analyse her emotions too
closely, nor question why the image of Azur, so vivid
that morning, had begun to fade so rapidly ever since
her lips had been seized by Torrin Anthony. It was
sometimes dangerous to ask too many questions.

He was leaning towards her and Merril felt his eyes
probing every nuance of her expression. 'That's the
second time you've called me Torrin,' he said eventually. 'It must be a good sign.' There was a kind of
catch in his voice that sent her mind spinning with the
wildness of its suppositions. But she knew he was a
master in the art of seduction, and anger, fiercely
controlled, welled in her throat. Why was he torment-
ing her like this? He received enough adulation, didn't
he, without trying to ensnare her heart too?

Dumbly she watched his thumb caressing the back of
her hand, then begin to inch its way inside her wrist
and along her forearm. It lingered agonisingly inside
the soft curve of her elbow and she became aware how
innocently erotic such a place could be beneath the
touch of an experienced lover. The thought made her
shiver with the feeling of desire he was arousing inside
her, and part of her wanted to yield to a more intimate
touch, to the sweetness of surrender. But her mind sent
out alarms, warning that he was simply using her,

trying to add yet another conquest in his insatiable
need for adulation.

With a tremendous effort of will she put out a hand
to stay his own, conscious of the rough hair on the
back of his arm and the bulk of muscle beneath the
skin.

'I don't know what game you're playing, Torrin, but
I don't want to join in.'

'No?' His voice was husky with emotion and she
marvelled at the skill with which he could manipulate
every inflection to imbue the simplest word with
layers of meaning. As he spoke his gentle caresses
continued, travelling to her shoulder, kneading out
the tension built by resistance, sending prickles of
desire all over her and making her long to yield.

'No!' she groaned, unable to hold back the yearning
note signalling her arousal. 'I don't want you to do
this. What does one more conquest matter to you?'

'I'm not counting, Merril. One is everything to me.'
His voice thickened with emotion. 'I've already told
you I'm an old-fashioned romantic when it comes to
love——'

'You're so plausible,' her voice seemed to come from
far away, 'but I can't believe a word you say.'

'The curse of my profession,' he murmured,
concentrating now on the curve of her jaw with an
assured touch that sent her desire spiralling.

'Why me?' She shuddered, clinging to the last
vestiges of resistance. 'You could have stayed in town
tonight with any one of those fans of yours. They
wouldn't resist.'

'Shall I show you why?' Torrin lifted his head. 'Shall
I?'

CHAPTER FIVE

MERRIL turned her head as he leaned towards her again, effectively pinning her against the pillows before she could move, his hard body weighing down on her, his face moving over her own, touching and not touching in a tantalising game of tag, lips circling, brushing, parting until she had to bite back the cry of desire blocking her throat, releasing it instead in a moan of fierce rage. 'It doesn't mean a thing!'

'No? You know you feel it. Come on, Merril, admit it. This is no dream. It's the real thing.'

She gave a shudder as she guessed that Torrin was making an oblique reference to what she had told him that afternoon about Azur. With a giant ego unable to bear the thought of any other competition, he was trying to make her forget her true love with all the seductive craft at his command.

'You'll never measure up to him,' she muttered feverishly, 'so don't waste time trying. You may have the same kind of physique——' a harsh laugh escaped her, for it was true, ragingly, painfully true, his body recalling such tender memories '—but in every other way you're much less of a man than he is.'

'Less in this way?' came the harsh rejoinder, his lips crushing down suddenly over hers, forcing her head back, prising her unwilling lips to open to him, hungrily, needily, gorging himself on her, his tongue searching fiercely for a response. Merril fought back, arching against him, aware that the duvet had slipped down and that she was pressing naked against the rough denim-clad body, but the force of his fingers raking through her hair, sliding with hot intensity down her silken skin, drawing her up into his arms, only slackened as he felt her yield. Then his kisses became less fierce, burning and pressing with a fine sensitivity, alive to each minute movement of desire. 'Less now?' he mocked, honey-brown eyes trailing hotly over her flushed cheeks.

Merril shuddered, knowing he could assess every quivering reaction to his touch.

Cold amusement seemed to line his face as he bent his head towards the satiny curve of her breasts. Her hands gripped compulsively at the powerful shoulders as his lips sought and found their goal, their touch whipping her to a peak of quivering joy. She wanted to cry out with longing, but despair at his calculated seduction swept her into a storm of confusioin. Biting back her longing, she pushed at his shoulders and, lifting his head, he said softly, 'Don't compare me to anyone again unless you want me to show you otherwise.'

He released her only to drag the cover over her naked breasts, then he crumpled her hands between one of his, trapping them, soothing her strangely by this gesture, eventually resting his head on the duvet, cocooning her within it. Oddly comforted, Merril felt her eyes begin to close at once. In a minute he would tell her why he had brought her here. She lay still, waiting, until with a small shock her eyes opened and, looking round, she realised she had drifted off to sleep. Torrin was still lying against her, eyes closed, breathing evenly, his head on her breasts. She strained to glimpse the bedside clock without disturbing him. Three twenty-nine, she saw. Her own eyes were closing drowsily again already as he shifted a little, burrowing down more comfortably into the pillows, dragging her closer still into the crook of his arm.

Sunlight was streaming across her face, making her roll on to her stomach to bury her head in the pillow. Then her eyes opened fully, sending her gaze swinging round the unfamiliar room. As it came into focus, the events of the previous night came flooding back, pulling her upright to stare at the empty space beside her.

So it hadn't been a dream. The hollow made by Torrin's body in the duvet was clearly visible. Thinking twice about spending the night with her, he had obviously returned to his own bed after she fell asleep . . .

Why had he failed to follow through with his obvious aim of adding yet one more conquest to his score? The answer was something she didn't want to know. It was frightening enough the way she had lost control. A past-master at seduction, he evidently knew just what to do to turn a woman on!

Showered and dried, she went back to her room to ready herself. A pink sweater and snug-fitting white jeans suited her slim figure. With blonde hair caught up in a casual topknot and a few escaping tendrils framing her face, she looked attractive. Yet she wasn't out to catch Torrin Anthony, unlike every other woman in London, so what did it matter what she looked like? All she wanted was material for an article and to escape as soon as possible.

The kitchen was empty when she went in, and she was settling down to her third cup of coffee when there was a sound and she looked up to see Torrin regarding her in amusement from the doorway.

'Feel rested now?' he asked, coming towards her as if he was about to give her a kiss on the cheek. Merril braced herself, but instead he went straight over to the fridge and took out a container of fruit juice.

'Come on, Merril, no slacking. I expected you to be up in the gym with me this morning, making notes,' he taunted.

'I would have been if I'd known where you were,' she replied, not really believing that was where he'd been. 'What's next on the agenda?'

'I have to look over some notes the director gave me last night. I'm afraid all this is going to be rather boring for you.'

'Never mind, it's all in the day's work,' she rejoined.

Torrin raised his eyebrows. 'Who knows, maybe we can provide a few surprises?' He laughed softly as she coloured at his suggestive tones.

'Don't bother,' she sparked back. 'You should know by now I'm not interested in any special performance you might be thinking of putting on.'

'No?' His yellow tiger's eyes slid lazily over her flushed face with a look of such indecent double meaning, she felt her cheeks burn an even brighter red. It was almost as if he could read what had flashed through her mind. She got up.

'This *is* what you want?' he asked, putting out a hand to touch her shoulder. 'I mean, for your article,' he added in a voice like dark velvet. His eyes lapped over her face, enjoying her confusion.

'"A day in the life of a star"—perfect!' she mocked, trying to keep a safe distance between them. 'It'll make interesting reading—the way *I* write it up!'

Without saying anything else, Torrin led the way into a small study off the living-room.

'Is this what you usually do on a Saturday?' she asked, striving to adopt a coolly professional manner as she sat down as far away from him as possible.

'No. I would probably stay in town and come out here on Sunday.'

'And what about any special routine——' She

paused, another maverick thought popping into her head.

'I cut down on some of the more taxing pleasures,' he remarked, picking up on it, 'drinking, parties——'

'Yes, I noticed,' Merril said hurriedly, not wishing to hear more. 'Since we met at a party I'll omit that, shall I?'

'Not at all. That one was the first-night party, so I had to be there. I left early.'

'Not before I did.'

'No, straight afterwards.' He looked as if he was about to say something else, but thought better of it and instead picked up his script.

The room they were in was tiny compared to the others in the rest of the house, but it was crammed with books from floor to ceiling—not all books, though, she corrected, giving the spines a quick scrutiny. Some were videos, nearly all of plays or musicals, or famous theatrical productions by well-known actors from the past.

'Is this where your ambitions lie?' she asked, pleased to be able to get on to something neutral and picking out a recording of *Hamlet*.

She saw Torrin pause before he replied, and when he gave a fairly non-committal response she pursed her lips. She shouldn't have felt irked by the fact that he obviously didn't trust her any more than she trusted him, and she knew she herself would have delivered the same response to a personal question like that, especially suspecting the answer would be headlined in all the tabloids.

Going back to one of the armchairs crammed between the beechwood desk and the french windows, she gave an audible sigh.

'It's not going to work if you censor my questions,' she remarked.

'Who's censoring anything?' Torrin demurred.

'You were just then.'

'Merril, there are some things I don't know the answer to,' he disarmed her with an apologetic shrug, 'and some things I won't discuss because they involve other people. Apart from that my life's an open book.'

'Other people?' She raised her eyebrows. 'A woman?'

He hesitated. 'Yes—yes, that's true. A woman.'

'It would be.'

'What can you mean?'

'There seem to be vast numbers of women in your life, Torrin,' she pointed out, striving to keep an unexpected snake of jealousy from surfacing.

He considered for a moment. 'Yes, I suppose that's true. Lots of 'em around, though. Even my karate teacher is a woman!'

'Karate?' she queried.

'Ex-world champion. Damn good teacher.'

Merril looked sceptical.

'She has a very tranquil quality,' he went on, after giving the matter some consideration. 'I appreciate that.'

'In a woman?'

'What is this? Yes, in a woman.' He thought a moment. 'And in a man, too. Useful to have somebody cool beside you when you're in a tight corner.'

'Are you?' she asked.

'What?'

'Ever in a tight corner where you need somebody cool beside you?'

'Frequently.'

She gave a scathing laugh, her thoughts with Azur for a moment. That was what she would call a tight corner—bullets whizzing overhead, Azur, cool as a cucumber through it all. 'You don't know the meaning of tight corners,' she observed dismissively.

'Oh, I don't know,' he spoke slowly. 'It gets pretty hairy on stage sometimes.'

'Yes, of course.' She gave him a pitying smile but didn't bother to explain it.

Something seemed to pass through his mind and then he scowled, adopting an expression she had never seen before. 'Are you trying to get at me because you've had a stint as a war correspondent and imagine it makes you eligible for the red badge?'

'Sorry?' She leaned forward.

'Oh, forget it.' His voice seemed to change, hardening somehow. 'You wouldn't understand the military allusion. Red badge of courage. Didn't you see the film? *True Grit*? Personally I like a woman to be all female—quiet, yielding, you know, submissive.' He turned his smile full on her, obviously unaware of her annoyance as he went on to expand this unexpected theme. 'A woman should be able to cook and look after her man, putting him first all the time. Nothing less will do for me. Career women?' He laughed. 'They leave me cold.'

This seemed so out of character, Merril could only gape. When he stopped she managed to say stiffly, 'Not all men agree with you these days.'

Torrin shook his head, looking sorrowfully out of the window. 'Pity. They'll rue it. When they look round for someone to sew a button on and there isn't a woman living who knows how to do it.'

'I don't believe I'm hearing this!'

'Take this rebel hero of yours, your comic strip Superman, what sort of woman do you imagine *he'll* want after a busy day at the front? He'll want a nice, soft kitten, Merril, not some hard-bitten career woman.'

Suddenly picking up a pen, he opened the script and began to read, shushing her when she tried to interrupt him, then suddenly getting up and leaving the room. Still seething, but assuming she was meant to follow him, Merril grabbed her notebook. He was already half-way up the stairs by the time she'd worked out where he'd gone. Tagging along after him, she saw him go into the gym, taking off his black track-suit to reveal a pair of red boxer shorts.

Despite her simmering fury she couldn't help but gape. He was even more impressive, physically, than she'd realised, with powerful shoulders, muscular chest and perfectly proportioned limbs, his thigh muscles bulging but not over-developed. His light tan was attractive against the bright gold of his cropped hair.

He turned briefly to gaze at her as if he didn't quite know who she was or what she was doing as she came inside, his face made stern by concentration, giving him a formidable air that had the effect of sending a spiral of fear through her. He looked as if he would cut her down to size as soon as look at her.

Concealing her anger at being put down, she opened her notebook with a display of hard-bitten efficiency he could either like or lump.

Inside she felt confused, disadvantaged by his chameleon quality. This morning he wasn't the same for two minutes together, and she couldn't help feeling it was deliberate. But what was she to make of those preposterous ideas of his? It had come after she had taunted him about tight corners, implying he wasn't much of a man. And that had come after she had expressed her thoughts about the number of women in his life . . . *Touché*, she thought. Now it looked as if he was deliberately trying to make her change her mind about his macho quotient!

After a few warm-up exercises Torrin went to the leg press and worked it hard with an impressive load of weights on board. Merril sighed; it was all so predictable.

Why did men imagine brute strength was impressive? It wasn't that that attracted her to Azur or made her respect her own father. It was an inner courage she admired, a feeling that here was a man who would never let her down.

She sat on a bench and watched. It had been a good idea of his to bring her out here, but not for the reasons he expected. She was getting the best possible insight into what made Torrin Anthony tick simply by watching him in action. It was worth hours of straight interviews of the question-and-answer variety.

Stifling a yawn, she started to doodle on the side of her pad. With luck he would take her back to town with him tonight, especially if she flattered him by asking if she could see the performance again. He would love the idea of her sitting in the wings drooling over him. She should have thought of it before. A man like this lapped up flattery like a cat with a bowl of cream.

Confident she had got his measure, and satisfied that she had managed to push the previous night back into perspective, she gave a start when a shadow fell across her pad.

'I hope that's not meant to be me?' Head on one side, Torrin gazed down at the series of concentric circles she had drawn.

'I couldn't do you justice,' she murmured suggestively, eyeing his near-naked body. Before she could move he flung a towel over his shoulders and went to the door.

'Have a work-out yourself while I'm in the shower,' he suggested over his shoulder. 'This part of the programme *is* censored——' Then he stopped, eyes roving wickedly over her face. 'Unless you insist, of course?'

'I—er—no, I don't think I'd be able to get it past my editor,' she answered coquettishly. When he went out she found her imagination focusing with disturbing insistence on what was taking place next door. It had been easier than she'd expected to let him think she was impressed.

The weather took a turn for the worse later that morning. Torrin had been out for a cross-country run and Merril had gamely accompanied him, grudgingly, but silently admiring when they finished to find that he was still as fresh as when he'd started, whereas she . . . 'Mind if I have a shower?' she asked, as she followed him up the steps into the house. Her anger was still simmering, despite the opportunity to run it off.

'Try the jacuzzi if you like. It'll stop your muscles aching tomorrow,' he suggested.

Stung to think he could see she had difficulty keeping up with him, she nodded and went up.

While she was splashing about in the swirling waters she heard the rain begin. The sound increased until it was pounding on the wooden roof of the millhouse with a deafening sound that cut out all else.

Getting out of the jacuzzi, she stood at the window and looked out. Water was already beginning to rage through the sluice out of the millpond, the stream in its steep cutting below the garden frothing over the lichen-covered rocks, twigs and small branches tossed up on a sudden wild journey downstream. The wooden bridge was high above the level of the water, and beyond that Merril could just glimpse the dark waters of the millpool itself, pitted with the lash of rain as the clouds opened. A strong smell of wet vegetation and rich earth mingled with the perfume of flowers. Then the wind veered, gusting in through the open window, bringing a spray of rain over her face. She wiped her eyes and dropped the catch.

She dressed and went back downstairs to find Torrin. He was waiting for her with a hot drink and smiled as she tasted it. 'It's a good pick-me-up. I use a lot of nervous energy when I'm in a show. Though I guess it looks effortless from the stalls—at least, I hope it does.'

'Oh, it does,' she agreed ironically. 'Everyone tells you so, don't they?'

'All the time. But then, as professional hangers-on that's their role, isn't it? In your view?'

She took another sip of the drink. 'It is rather good,' she admitted with unexpected relish. Then she gave a sudden laugh, her eyes alight. 'But don't take that as flattery, will you?'

'As if I would,' Torrin murmured drily, his amber eyes drifting over her face, suddenly stopping, lingering over her smiling mouth with such a look of desire that the breath was trapped in her throat and a deep stillness held them both in its grip; it was as if everything in the universe had swung to a momentary halt.

Merril tried to turn away but couldn't, and stood transfixed as he moved slowly towards her.

'When you relax, when you stop sparring with me and forget all your preconceptions, you have a look of such openness—innocence . . .' Cautiously he lifted one hand and reached forward towards her. 'Merril . . . you're so beautiful.'

She took a shuddering breath. Outside the rain was still pounding on the roof, but here within they were locked in a half-lit world of their own. It was a moment out of time as Torrin's hand, slowly reaching out, touched her hair, her face, hovering, sliding with feather lightness down the side of her cheek to her lips, and his voice honeyed over her, saying, 'Let's stop fighting and start loving. I want you so much, darling, so very much . . .'

CHAPTER SIX

THE ROOM had darkened now as the storm passed right overhead. They were rain-locked in an island of their own. Merril felt anything could happen. Hypnotised by the indescribable softness of Torrin's touch, she struggled to regain her detachment, desperately striving like someone in a dream to return to a state of wakefulness.

Moving her head slightly in an attempt to free herself from the whisper of his touch on her pulsing skin, she heard her own voice utter a single cry of protest.

'Don't fight me, Merril,' he replied.

'Yes——' she croaked, her mind a turmoil of emotion. 'I must. You're not—you're not the sort of man I could ever—please, Torrin, don't touch me like that!'

'I don't fit the image of your ideal lover?' he mocked, letting his fingers slide into her hair as if she hadn't objected.

'Lover, perhaps,' she came back, surprised to find it was true. 'But when I give myself it'll be for ever . . . to a man I can respect as well as desire. Nothing less will do!' Her eyes skidded helplessly over his handsome features and down the tanned column of his neck to the powerful shoulders, to the broad chest, aware of the perfect physique beneath the designer denims, then back, helplessly, to lock once more with those knowing amber eyes, fighting what they were telling her with such engulfing power.

His voice was soft but full of conviction. 'You're

The more you love romance . . . the more you'll love this offer

FREE!

Mail this heart today! (See inside)!

Join us on a Harlequin Honeymoon and we'll give you

4 free books

A free bracelet watch

And a free mystery gift

IT'S A
HARLEQUIN HONEYMOON—
A SWEETHEART
OF A FREE OFFER!
HERE'S WHAT YOU GET:

1. **Four New Harlequin Presents® Novels—FREE!**
   Take a Harlequin Honeymoon with your four exciting romances—yours FREE from Harlequin Reader Service®. Each of these hot-off-the-press novels brings you the passion and tenderness of today's greatest love stories . . . your free passports to bright new worlds of love and foreign adventure.

2. **A Lovely Bracelet Watch—FREE!**
   You'll love your elegant bracelet watch—this classic LCD quartz watch is a perfect expression of your style and good taste—and it is yours FREE as an added thanks for giving our Reader Service a try.

3. **An Exciting Mystery Bonus—FREE!**
   You'll be thrilled with this surprise gift. It is elegant as well as practical.

4. **Money-Saving Home Delivery!**
   Join Harlequin Reader Service® and enjoy the convenience of previewing eight new books every month delivered right to your home. Each book is yours for only $2.24*—26¢ less per book than the cover price. And there is *no* extra charge for postage and handling. Great savings plus total convenience add up to a sweetheart of a deal for you! If you're not completely satisfied, you may cancel at any time, for any reason, simply by sending us a note or shipping statement marked "cancel" or by returning any shipment to us at our cost.

5. **Free Insiders' Newsletter**
   It's *heart to heart*®, the indispensible insiders' look at our most popular writers, upcoming books, even comments from readers and much more.

6. **More Surprise Gifts**
   Because our home subscribers are our most valued readers, when you join the Harlequin Reader Service®, we'll be sending you additional free gifts from time to time—as a token of our appreciation.

START YOUR HARLEQUIN HONEYMOON TODAY—JUST
COMPLETE, DETACH AND MAIL YOUR FREE-OFFER CARD

DETACH AND MAIL TODAY!

PLACE
HEART STICKER
HERE

GIVE YOUR HEART
TO HARLEQUIN

YES! Please send me my four Harlequin Presents® novels FREE, along with my free bracelet watch and free mystery gift. I wish to receive all the benefits of the Harlequin Reader Service® as explained on the opposite page.

NAME _____
(PLEASE PRINT)

ADDRESS _____ APT. _____

CITY _____ STATE _____

ZIP CODE _____

108 CIH CAPA (U-H-P-09/89)

OFFER LIMITED TO ONE PER HOUSEHOLD AND NOT VALID TO CURRENT HARLEQUIN PRESENTS® SUBSCRIBERS.

HARLEQUIN READER SERVICE® "NO RISK" GUARANTEE

— There's no obligation to buy—and the free books and gifts remain yours to keep.
— You pay the low members-only discount price and receive books before they appear in stores.
— You may end your subscription anytime by sending us a note or shipping statement marked "cancel" or by returning any shipment to us at our cost.

PRINTED IN U.S.A.
© 1989 HARLEQUIN ENTERPRISES LIMITED

If offer card is missing, write to: Harlequin Reader Service® 901 Fuhrmann Blvd
P.O. Box 1867 Buffalo NY 14269-1867

BUSINESS REPLY CARD

FIRST CLASS MAIL   PERMIT NO. 717   BUFFALO, NY

POSTAGE WILL BE PAID BY ADDRESSEE

HARLEQUIN READER SERVICE
901 FUHRMANN BLVD
PO BOX 1867
BUFFALO NY 14240-9952

NO POSTAGE
NECESSARY
IF MAILED
IN THE
UNITED STATES

DETACH AND MAIL TODAY!

stuck with some fantasy figure and it won't let you
see the real man in front of you. Wake up to reality,
Merril. Let me show you the difference between a
flesh-and-blood lover and this impossible ideal
you've invented. You'll forget your dream lover
when you have the real thing.'

'Real thing?' she exclaimed, her voice rising as she
struggled to resist what he was telling her. 'Is
anything real for you? Even now I don't know
whether you're acting or not!' She broke off with a
harsh laugh. 'But I do know, don't I? That's one
thing I *can* be sure of!'

His eyes were dark hollows. She felt menaced by
the look in them, as if she could read there a threat to
take away all her resistance.

Torrin held out a hand. 'Believe in me, Merril,' he
said simply. 'This is real.' Panic sent her stepping
back, dashing his hand away, terrified to find herself
on the verge of betraying the past.

'Don't touch me!' she repeated, gaining strength
from the deep well of fear on whose brink she stood.
'I hate everything you stand for! Nothing you say is
true. You're a sham! Your whole life is a masquerade!
You want to see me surrender because I resist. Vanity
won't let you leave me in peace. You can't see I don't
want anything to do with you. I'm only here because
my editor forced me to take this stupid assignment. I
didn't want to interview you. I hate you! I hate
everything you stand for!'

A flash of lightning lit p the room, giving his face
an unearthly look, making it haggard, hollow-eyed,
like a mask. Her words sounded thin against the roar
of the storm, but she tried to inject conviction into the
words she flung at him by raising her voice. 'There's
only one kind of man I want—and it's not your kind!
Call it a dream—I don't care!' As she spoke she
almost believed she was as indifferent as she claimed.

Her face was a white oval in the half-light.

'You little fool!' Torrin ground out, all gentleness wiped out in a sudden surge of violence. 'Can't you see the truth even now?' He lunged towards her and she gave a small scream, stumbling back out of range, felt his arms come round her, crushing her against his hard body, fury sparking from him like a powerful current, paralysing her for a moment until she rallied, flinging back her head with a harsh laugh of scorn at this perfectly enacted image of a man in torment.

'Still acting, Torrin? But this is real life. You're not on stage now! Can't you tell the difference?'

She felt his grasp slacken. In the darkness his face looked ashen, drained of colour by the weird storm-light filtering through the windows. She twisted, glimpsing the thrashing branches of the trees outside as the deluge flattened them, expecting him to release her. But instead his hands tightened round her waist, his desire blazingly real as he ground her body against his own.

Suddenly the helplessness she felt in his arms arrowed through her again with sickening speed. He could, he would take her, despite her protests, her struggles, her cries for help. She would be unable to stop him. His desire was real, animal, overwhelming. His face, a perfect mask of desire, made her tremble with fear.

Then the real danger scored her mind. It wasn't Torrin's desire she was afraid of—it was her own, her own wild, savage yearning to be taken, to be loved, to give herself completely to the fire consuming her soul.

With a shuddering breath she forced herself to slacken her struggles, feeling his own hold loosen as he thought she was about to yield, then with a panic-stricken twist she was out of his arms and half-way across the room before he could follow. She pushed a chair into his path as he lunged after her, seeing with satisfaction how he stumbled for a moment, giving her sufficient time to wrench open the door.

Then she was running, mindlessly, heedlessly, through the torrential downpour, across the garden, towards the wooden bridge.

She reached it just as Torrin ran down the steps, her name on his lips, the sound ringing out eerily in the persistent crashing of the water along the bottom of the cut.

With one last flinging look over her shoulder she reached out for the bridge rail, then to her immense horror she grasped air, her feet skidding under her on the wet stones at the brink of the stream, and then she was falling, twisting, hitting the bank half-way down, then rolling over, scrabbling helplessly at the mud bank, fingers grasping uselessly at trailing stems as they broke beneath her grasp, gasping as the shock of cold water ran rapidly up inside her blouse, closing with the finality of a door above her head.

The next few seconds were a blank, until she was thrown to the surface further downstream, an image beneath the surface of her panic of Torrin standing at the top of the bank. Then fear took over as the current sucked her down, drawing the waters over her like a suffocating veil.

It was a familiar voice, not her own, intimately near, a whirl of white and a tangle of restraining threads pulling at her, that made her start fighting, lashing out, feeling only empty space, then something heavy, dragging at her limbs, filling her mouth so that her breath felt stopped. Then her eyes opened fully. Torrin was leaning over her.

For a moment she wondered if he had carried out his earlier intention, and she sat up in panic, surprised to find herself lying in thick wet grass and not in the bed she had immediately imagined. Confused, she looked about her.

'Keep still, you're a little concussed.' His arm was round her for support. It felt right like that. Merril lay back for a moment, her eyes struggling to close against her determination to keep them open.

Familiar lines flitted into her mind and she gave a weak laugh. 'At the risk of sounding corny, where . . .' Her words trailed away with the effort.

'Where are you?' Torrin finished, holding her close. 'You slipped into the millrace. Not the best time to go swimming when it's as swollen as it is now,' he reproved gently as he smoothed back her wet hair and pulled a a few leaves out of it. 'You look like a mermaid, a siren. Can you sing?'

'Not at the moment.' Forcing her eyes open, Merril blinked up at him through small slits. The light hurt. But it was surprisingly pleasant lying here with him in the grass. She nestled against him. All she could remember was their argument in the house, his rugged body overwhelmingly close, her own feeling of wanting to yield to its power . . .

'Was that why I ran away?' she murmured, trying to sit up a little.

'What's that, darling?'

It seemed natural for him to address her with such intimate tenderness. 'I ran away because I thought—I thought——'

'I know what you thought.' His face was so close to her own that she could see the faint hardening in his eyes, the compression of his long, mobile lips, and she reached out to touch them.

'Your lips are so heavenly,' she murmured.

'Heavenly, are they now?' He looked down at her. 'That's not what you've been trying to tell me for the last day or so. It takes a knock on the head, does it?'

She moved her face closer, tilting her lips so that

they nearly brushed his, waiting expectantly for the ravishing warmth of their touch on her own. But he simply shifted his arm so that she was moved a little out of range.

'Your clothes are all wet, even your hair . . .' She brushed her fingers over the wet stubble.

'I haven't yet devised a way of moving through water without getting wet,' Torrin told her, catching her fingers as they hovered near his lips.

She gave him a wondering look. 'You mean you dived into the millrace and dragged me to safety?'

'Of course I did, you little idiot. You didn't expect me to stand helplessly on the bank and let you drown, did you?'

The brief lowering of her lashes was eloquent enough.

'Thanks.' He tucked her hand by her side and let it go.

'Do you feel you can get up now?' he asked curtly. 'I don't want to get a streaming cold from sitting in wet grass when I've got a show to do.'

Ignoring this, Merril leaned against him, letting him haul her to her feel after a moment or two, pressing herself close against him as they stood. Their faces were only a few inches apart. She felt her chin tilt again, hungry for the touch that before she had fiercely resisted.

'Can you walk? Come on, try,' he urged, ignoring her undulations as she leaned against him.

They were on the edge of a meadow bordering the stream beneath the level of the garden, and he helped her walk slowly back through lush grass spotted with celandines, as yellow bright as Chinese lacquer, and made misty beneath a distant hawthorn hedge by a haze of cow parsley. The place had a tremulous beauty to match Merril's feelings.

Weakly she leaned against him, giving up any

pretence that the touch of his body didn't arouse her own to a fever of desire. But he forced her to keep walking even when, as they climbed the slope to the house, her feet slipped and he had to hold her tightly in his arms.

She almost convinced herself it was the prelude to a scene like the one in the house. This time, she knew, things would be different. She felt vulnerable, quivering with tenderness, sorry from the bottom of her heart for the hateful things she had said to him. Her antagonism had been overrun by all the mixed-up emotions her discovery of her true feelings and the accident and Torrin's rescue had aroused.

He was leading her with painful slowness across the garden, so slowly she was becoming impatient.

'Go in,' he said when they reached the steps. 'Have a hot shower. Can you manage by yourself?' He looked up at her from the bottom of the steps.

She must have registered puzzlement, for he gave a faint smile. 'I'll be with you in a moment. Go on, do as I say.'

Puzzled, Merril went in alone, squelching over the parquet to the stairs, dropping her sodden clothes down on the Spanish tiles in the bathroom as soon as she could discard them, thankful that Torrin's austerity didn't exclude the very latest in bathroom equipment. Before her accident this indulgence would have been one more mark against him. Now she was ready to revise her opinion in one sweep. How she had misjudged him! her thoughts ran on as she stood under the shower. She had been convinced he would be the type to lose his head at the slightest hint of physical danger, but he had proved her wrong, risking his own life to save hers.

'You're still in shock. I wonder if that bump on your head needs attention?'

A voice from the doorway lifted her head. She had

emerged from the shower, dragging one of the red towels round herself, and remembered sitting on the edge of the bath for a moment. She must have been there longer than she realised. Now Torrin was staring at her from the doorway, not with the brightness of desire in his eyes, but with a look of deep concern. She allowed the towel to slip a little, revealing one breast, longing to see the look of desire in his eyes once more. She was chilled when he merely reached out, pulling down a bathrobe from behind the door and flinging it over her with a curt, 'Put that on, then go to your room. I'll bring you a drink.'

A few minutes later Merril was propped up against a mound of lacy pillows, a glass of brandy in her hand, Torrin lying across the foot of the bed in a black towelling bathrobe, his tanned face turned away from her as he spoke.

'I can't leave you here by yourself. When you feel rested you'd better get dressed and come into town with me this evening. You can sit in my dressing-room during the performance, and if you need anything my dresser will be on hand to help you.'

It was exactly what she had wanted earlier, an excuse to get back to London, to make her escape. But now she had no intention of running away. She would stay with Torrin—she had to, because he had revealed a side of his character she hadn't suspected. She wanted to see more of it. She had made a mistake about him, as well as about the depth of her own feelings. When he had dragged her out of the millrace there was no way he could have been acting. For the first time she was convinced he was genuine. The courage to risk one's own neck in order to rescue someone in danger was not something that could ever be faked.

The car arrived just after five to pick Torrin up for the theatre, and Merril, ready to go, was first out of the house.

She was half-way towards the bridge before she slowed, turning impatiently as Torrin seemed to take an age to walk down the steps and follow her across the garden towards it.

'Frightened?' he gibed when he eventually came up beside her.

'Not with you here,' she replied, adding, 'You're the one who looks frightened. Are you all right? You're as white as a sheet!'

'I'm always frightened. I thought that's what you had against me?' he responded with a cutting glance.

'Stage fright?' she questioned, astonished, but able to think of no other explanation.

'That as well,' he replied cryptically. 'A lot of actors suffer stage fright.' He pushed her ahead. 'Don't hang about. I like to have plenty of time to endure the agony before the half-hour call.'

Not sure whether he meant to be taken seriously or not, Merril did as she was told, hurrying with a certain nervous care across the narrow bridge towards the oak grove and the waiting car.

The driver greeted them both with a flash of white teeth, and slipped the car smoothly into first gear as soon as they were inside.

Torrin seemed to lapse into a sort of trance through the journey, and she dared not disturb him until they came within sight of the theatres along the Strand an hour later. The cloudburst that had descended on the millhouse had transformed the streets of London to dark mirrors, reflecting the glitter of coloured lights, bright jewels, sparkling along their route. Something of the excitement of the West End on a Saturday night gripped Merril then, and she turned excitedly as they passed the theatre with Torrin's name in lights for everyone to see.

A feeling of pride ran through her unexpectedly and she felt a twinge of guilt for belittling his success. He had a right to be conceited if any man had, though now she really thought about it there were few signs of arrogance in his character. Self-confidence, perhaps, but not conceit. Nothing his success didn't warrant. She had been mean-minded towards him and it was like scales falling from her eyes to understand that. Soon she would tell him so, and she would make amends for that terrible outburst at the millhouse.

The car dropped them outside the stage door, and even at this early hour a knot of fans stood outside in the rain, surging forward with little cries of delight as soon as they recognised Torrin. He signed their autograph books, thanked them with a modest shrug for their extravagant comments on his performance, then hustled inside past the stage doorkeeper with one arm under Merril's elbow as if to make sure she didn't escape. In fact, he was leaning on her almost as if he required her support.

'Are you going to be all right?' he asked her once they were safely within the ill-lit corridor backstage.

'Everything seems unreal—no, I mean more real. Odd, though. Different,' she admitted, confused by his glance. 'I'm seeing things differently now,' she added with a meaningful smile.

'I'll get Tom to call the theatre doctor,' Torrin told her, pushing her on ahead of him. 'Go in.'

Put out that he had misunderstood what she was trying to say, Merril pushed open the door into the dressing-room where she had met him two days ago. It was empty now, but there were signs of someone's presence, with a full-length fake fur slung over a sofa against the far wall. The bulbs round the make-up mirror were on and a man's voice singing a song from the show came from behind them as they went inside.

'Not before time, darlings, where *have* you been?'

A small, dark man of indeterminate age came into the room.

'Merril, meet Tom, my dresser——'

'And general factotum—hello, darling, you're as beautiful as you were the other night in that glorious pink dress. Whatever happened to you at the party? You seemed to vanish into thin air. Tor hasn't forgiven me for letting you slip away like that.'

'Shut up, Tommy, we've had a bit of an accident.' Torrin's face was like a thundercloud. 'Call the doctor, if you can bear to stop talking long enough to do anything useful, and tell him to come over at once.'

'He's already in, darling. Lydia's been having throat trouble *as* predicted.' Tom sighed extravagantly and shrugged his shoulders. 'She must have caught that throat bug you had when you were away. You had a voice like a corncrake when you came back, so if she's got it too, God help us all!' He turned to Merril. 'And what have *we* been up to that warrants the attentions of Dr Foster?'

'Merril had an unscheduled swim at the mill and was a little concussed by the time she climbed out,' explained Torrin, not altogether accurately. 'We don't want her passing out on us, do we? I'm counting on you to take good care of her while I'm working.'

'What's one more swooning female to us, sweetie?' Despite his words Tom gave her a sympathetic smile and went off down the corridor, taking up his song where he had left off, and presumably going in search of the doctor.

'Take no notice of anything he says,' warned Torrin, avoiding her glance. 'He's totally over the top sometimes.' He removed the fake fur and settled Merril down on the sofa. 'I have to get changed now. Don't talk to me unless you have to. I'm not used to having anyone in my dressing-room before a performance—except Tom, of course, and he knows better than to get in my way.'

It was a relief to lie down. Her near-drowning had

shaken her up more than she realised, and the turmoil of emotion that had ensued had made her feel exhausted, so she lay back and let Torrin tuck a blanket in around her, closing her eyes and only opening them when Tom came back in again. The two men didn't speak to each other at all, but they worked as a team, Tom laying out all the things Torrin needed and Torrin himself working methodically and routinely at the task of turning himself into an eighteenth-century rake.

Merril watched, fascinated, as the face in the mirror was slowly transformed. It was strangely erotic to see the familiar masculine features enhanced and subtly altered by the application of eye-liner, white pancake, shadows, and finally the black wig. Their eyes met briefly in the glass. Torrin's were blank, dark sockets, Merrill's blue, glistening with love. Seeing them, she knew then what he could read in them. It was plain to anyone what she was feeling.

'Coming up to the half, love,' said Tom, breaking into her reverie. Torrin rose to his feet, wincing as he stepped forward.

'It's nothing, a bruise or something from this afternoon,' he explained as Tom gave him a quizzical glance. He went out.

Tom looked at Merril rather suspiciously after he'd gone, and, busying himself with tidying away Torrin's theatrical make-up, he told her, 'It's tough at the beginning, before a show settles into its stride. We all try to protect each other to make sure nobody blows it by letting their personal life affect their performance.' He blew powder off the back of a hand mirror. 'It's particularly hard for Torrin, as he carries the whole show.'

'I take it that's some sort of warning?' she asked, playing with the fringe of the tartan blanket she had been wrapped up in.

'Take it as you choose. Tor would have my guts for garters if he imagined I was warning off his lady-friends.'

'I suppose he has plenty of those,' she muttered, unhappily aware of how little she knew of his personal life.

'Yes, what do you expect?' Tom eyed her pale face. 'Oh, I am a beast! You look absolutely jiggered, poor darling. Here, would you like a tot of brandy?' He went to a cupboard and took down a glass and a bottle. 'Medicinal purposes only. Tor won't have a sip before a show—he's a real puritan. But it obviously pays off. You saw the first night, didn't you? Wasn't he out of this world? I've been telling everyone for years how wonderful he is, but nobody's woken up to the fact till now. But praise be, it's happened at last. If anybody deserves it, he does. Here—sip it slowly. Don't throw it back or he'll be accusing me of trying to get you drunk.'

Merril did as she was told and submitted to her blanket being neatened up along with the rest of the room. 'There now,' said Tom when he'd finished, 'Doctor should be along in a minute. I'm going to put my feet up while I've got the chance. It's mayhem in here during the change.' So saying, he draped himself in a chair with his feet on a corner of the dressing-table and opened a magazine.

'You can listen to the show if you like. Press that switch there. That's right,' he nodded as Merril did as he directed. 'Now you can drool over his heavenly voice,' he added with a friendly leer.

The doctor's visit coincided with Torrin's brief period off-stage during the second act. Merril was shocked by his appearance. Underneath the white make-up his face seemed hollowed and he collapsed on to the end of the sofa, nearly crushing her legs before she could get them out of the way. Tom was on his feet at once.

'Who wanted me?' said the doctor, looking from

Merril to Torrin.

'He does.' It was Tom. He was peering into Torrin's face, his own face wreathed with concern.

'Look at Merril first,' protested Torrin. 'She was concussed earlier this afternoon.'

The doctor gave her a routine going over. 'Nothing that another stiff brandy won't cure,' he announced. Then he looked at Torrin.

'It's nothing much. I think I've cricked my ankle. I just need to sit down for a minute or two.' He leaned back, trying to look at ease. But the doctor wasn't to be put off. 'Let's have the boot off. Which foot is it?'

Torrin held out his right leg. Tom took hold of the heel and gently eased the boot off. Gentle though he was, Merril could feel Torrin wince with pain, both hands clenched and beads of perspiration dripping down his forehead even though it wasn't a particularly hot evening.

Now she saw why he had walked back so slowly from the riverbank and had taken his time about crossing the bridge as they left. Dr Foster's face looked grave. 'You've fractured it, by the look of things. Does it hurt?'

'Only when I jump on it.'

The doctor gave him a quick glance to see if he was joking, decided he wasn't, and adopted an admonitory stance. 'I know it's no use telling you to put it up for a few days—I remember you after that parachuting accident.' He sighed. 'It's like whistling in the wind. I'll give you a painkiller, then I want you to let me strap it up for you. If I were you I'd pop into Casualty and let them do it properly after the show. Won't be able to put your boots on——'

Torrin gave an exclamation of disgust. 'Look, I'm on in a minute.' He got up, reaching out for Tom's arm, and hopping about on one leg in an attempt to get the boot back on to the now visibly swelling ankle.

The doctor, taking something from his black bag, gave Tom a look of desperation. 'Can't you talk sense into him?'

The voice of the stage manager came over the speaker. 'Act Two, Scene Three beginners, please.'

'That's me,' muttered Torrin.

'Take these, then, unless you want to pass out on stage,' ordered the doctor.

'Will they slow me up?'

'I doubt it. They're not horse pills.' The doctor, evidently admitting defeat, retreated into mild sarcasm. 'I'll be waiting for you when you come off—or when they carry you off, whichever's the sooner,' he added, patting him on the back. Torrin gulped down the painkillers and, the boot now crushed back on, was already at the door.

'Oh, hell,' muttered Merril, unable to help herself after he'd gone. 'It's all my fault.' Then she blurted out to Tom what had happened that afternoon, omitting the reason for her sudden dash towards the bridge, but finishing up in a small voice, with the words, 'No wonder he's being cool towards me if it means he can't go on next week. He's really going to hate me!'

'Darling, we'll all hate you, the entire universe will hate you if he can't go on next week. Without him the show is just another moderately successful West End hit. With him it's the best thing to have happened in the world of theatre for decades. I shall personally strangle you if he's in any way prevented from going on next week. My God! That this should happen now!'

Then he surprised her by chucking her under the chin. 'Cheer up, sweetheart. The only thing that would stop Tor from setting foot on stage is if the roof fell in. He's had far worse injuries than this in his time, and it hasn't made a scrap of difference. The man's impervious to pain. He's not like us ordinary mortals. Fear not, I won't be getting an excuse to strangle you just yet. And make sure I never do. I'm like a raging animal defending its young when it comes to protecting Tor Anthony from the hordes of ravening scalp-hunters with which his path is habitually strewn. You don't look like one of that breed, but who knows? One can't be too careful.'

Merril bit her lip, not quite sure how to take Tom's warning, then she began to giggle. 'You don't like me at all, do you, Tom? I'm quite nice when you get to know me. And if you need any help against the scalp-hunters, all you have to do is whistle. I'd like to see them routed too!'

'Yes, I bet you would, you naughty girl.'

'He is gorgeous, isn't he, Tommy? I didn't trust him at all when I first met him. I thought he was just another egomaniac of an actor—all show and no substance. I felt I couldn't believe a word he said to me. I've never met anybody quite like him before.'

'And you won't, my poppet. Don't treat him lightly—he's an original.' They exchanged smiles, and for the first time that evening Merril began to feel she had an ally.

CHAPTER SEVEN

DR FOSTER was waiting in the wings for Torrin as the final curtain fell. Merril had slipped out of the dressing-room after him. Tom, following the action on stage through the speaker, had already gone ahead, his face showing concern.

There had been too many curtain calls and Torrin had gone back again and again, his electric smile vividly in place, with no outward sign of the pain he must have been suffering. When the audience finally released him he allowed the two men to help him back to his dressing-room. Feeling helpless, Merril trailed along behind, wanting nothing more than to put her arms around his broad shoulders and tell him how wonderful he was. But other things came first.

He collapsed at once on to the sofa, arms out along the back of it, and extended his right boot. 'Do your worst, Foster.'

First a knife had to be found, sharp enough to cut away the thick leather as it was now impossible to pull it over the swollen ankle. Torrin exchanged a constant patter with Tom over the doctor's head as the job was quickly carried out. Merril turned away with a little gasp when she saw Torrin's red and swollen ankle, visibly throbbing as the blood pulsed through it. Dr Foster didn't say anything, but he gave Torrin a look that plainly told him he thought he was a fool to have gone on stage that evening.

Even now the audience could be heard over the speaker, the applause like the regular rise and fall of surf upon a distant beach, and Torrin looked as if he was having second thoughts about coming off so soon, but the doctor got to work at once, giving him no option but to lie back and give in.

His eyes seemed to darken as the fingers probed along the fractured bones, but his only sign of pain was when he lifted a hand and said irritably, 'Take this damned wig, Tommy.'

Merril's heart went out to him as she watched him drop his head back, cropped hair longer than when she had first seen him. Now she wanted to caress him, smooth away his pain, run her fingers through the short, rumpled blond strands. Despite the brocade jacket and flowing shirt, his masculinity was tantalisingly enhanced, sending spirals of desire racing through her body.

'I'm going to have to get some new boots from somewhere. Will you see to it, Tom?' she heard him ask.

'Will do.'

'You'll have your ankle strapped up. You'll have to have them fitted over it,' the doctor warned.

'No problem,' said Tom, taking charge. 'Marie's already gone, but I'll give her a ring first thing in the morning. Can you stay in town tonight, for a fitting tomorrow?'

'Make it early. I want to have a nice relaxing Sunday.'

'Yes. Rest up,' advised the doctor, giving Torrin a suspicious glance. 'No flying, understand?'

Merril was amazed to see Torrin actually look evasive. 'Who? Me?' he asked, quickly changing the subject. 'Merril, is that all right?' He gave her a hurried glance and she nodded, but he was already making some joke to Tom and their eyes didn't meet, and she suddenly felt left out, not knowing half the people they were talking about, nor understanding all their in-jokes.

Torrin still seemed distant, hardly looking at her, and certainly not making any attempt to include her in their light-hearted banter, but she put it down to the racking pain he must be in, and admired him even more for treating it with so little concern. He was tough—maybe not as tough as Azur or her father, but he had the sort of courage she admired. Honesty forced her to admit she should have suspected as much from the first. She would tell him as soon as they were alone.

Dr Foster had just finished his task when there was a knock on the door and a woman's voice called, 'Are you decent, darling?' It swung open to reveal a tall, dark-haired woman, glossily made-up, a dazzling smile on her face. 'Sweetie, so it is true! I thought you were a little slow on the turn at the end of my court speech. You poor, poor darling!'

Making much of her entrance, she paused dramatically until all eyes were on her, then she moved into Torrin's arms, extending her graceful body alongside his on the couch. 'They said you'd done something to yourself, but I couldn't believe them. Why on earth didn't you mention it? We could have propped you in an armchair for the whole of the last act.'

'Yes, you would, too,' smiled Torrin, evidently pleased to be petted by so glamorous a female. One of his arms slipped around her shoulders.

'Anything to steal the show, Lydia darling,' quipped Tom. 'But even you have to wait until he's crippled.'

'I wouldn't risk it, otherwise,' she laughed throatily. 'We've decided to whisk you away to a nightclub.' She gave Torrin a critical look. 'Yes, I think that might do the trick. Just what the doctor ordered.'

'You might be, Lydia, but he doesn't always take his medicine,' rejoined Tom. He came to stand over Torrin with folded arms.

Torrin gave Lydia a rueful shrug. ' "Another time", he's trying to say.'

'Tom, you're a bossy beast. You come with us, anyway. Or do you have to nanny darling Tory?'

Darling Tory! thought Merril, saying nothing. She found Tom's eyes on her.

'I think he's fixed up in that department.' He raised his eyebrows, but Torrin cut in with a curt, 'I'm not in the mood for a lot of fuss. I'm going to have a good night's sleep, got to get another pair of boots fixed by Wardrobe first thing——' He looked exhausted as he spoke, and Merril wanted to clear the lot of them out of his room and let him get out of his stage clothes and into something more comfortable. Can't they see he needs rest? she thought helplessly.

Tom must have had the same idea. Several other members of the cast called by, but he did staunch duty at the door to keep out the autograph-hunters and the fans and other visitors backstage, and eventually Torrin managed to get his dressing-room back to himself. He removed his make-up and started to get changed, struggling a little as he tried to balance on one leg to put his trousers on.

'You're getting a real fly-on-the-wall view,' he muttered as he reached over Merril for a jacket that she could quite easily have passed to him herself. There was still something unfriendly in his tone, but when he turned to field some comment of Tom's the old hundred-watt smile was in place again and she thought she must have imagined that brief lowering of the temperature as he addressed her.

'That new chap on the stage door has booked your hotel, love.' Tom, complete with fake fur, gave a last housewifely inspection of the room.

'Thanks.' Ready to leave himself, Torrin limped to the door. 'Ring me there in the morning. Early, Tom, don't forget. I want to get back to the millhouse as soon as I can.'

They didn't leave by the stage door because Tom

went on ahead and warned them there was a crowd of about fifty standing outside under umbrellas waiting to catch a glimpse of Torrin. So instead they went out through the darkened front of house, red plush and gilt giving way to the cool green and gold of the foyer. Torrin managed to limp the few yards down the Strand to their hotel, and when they reached reception he leaned on the desk, trying to disguise the fact that it had been an ordeal, Merril observed tenderly.

She waited by the lift as he suggested, but even from there she could see that something was wrong. Torrin said something to the receptionist and she was shrugging apologetically, but when he rejoined her he didn't explain. Only when he came to unlock the door of their suite did he admit there had been a mistake.

'They've given us a double room, but don't worry, you'll be safe. There's a day bed in it.' He switched on the lights and looked round.

It was a first-class suite—peach brocade, floor-length curtains, mirrors everywhere, reproduction antique furniture, huge vases of hothouse flowers—and a sumptuous double bed dominating the main room.

'You can put all this in your article,' he told Merril drily.

'Is there anything I can get you?' she asked, ignoring that gibe and hovering round him, not sure how best to make herself useful.

'Not a damn thing. And don't play Florence Nightingale. I'm not in the mood.'

'Sorry.'

'And don't be sorry.'

'Sorry, I mean——'

'Just go to bed. It's been a hell of a day.' He limped over to the day bed and began to rearrange the cushions.

'But, Torrin, I have to say I'm sorry. I mean——' Merril broke off as he turned his head with an impatient jerk as if to cut her off. 'I mean, I'm sorry for what I said at the millhouse and for making you injure your ankle——'

'Don't feel you have to put on a show of feminine sympathy at this stage. It's quite out of character.'

'I'm not, I mean—it's not a show.'

'It's the real thing?' His voice was harsh.

She flinched. 'Yes,' she whispered, her throat going dry.

'Impressive, but ill-timed,' he observed coldly. 'Save it for somebody else.'

He was already stripping off his shirt and didn't notice her sharp intake of breath. It was becoming familiar to see him without many clothes but he never failed to dazzle her. She took a step forward, but he was ignoring her again, so she sank down on the side of the bed farthest away from him and began to take off her stockings. Everything was wrong. She was confused, didn't know what she wanted, but she knew it wasn't this. Torrin's rejection was unexpected, chilling her to the bone. And why was she always in these compromising situations with him? Why couldn't their relationship develop like any other? Words Tom had spoken came back to her: 'He's an orginal.' And she kicked her shoes under the bed with a little spurt of anger, wishing for something, but not sure what.

A voice from behind made her turn. 'I can't get these damned jeans back over the stuff Foster put on.' He gave a helpless look, dark eyes flicking over her face, noticing her blushes. He was sitting in nothing but his underpants, and her startled expression must have been plain. It seemed to amuse him.

'It's all right,' she muttered, embarrassed, 'I'll help.' As she pulled the offending garment away, Torrin started to chuckle softly.

'I've never taken your finer feelings into account,

have I? In my job I get used to clothes coming off at the drop of a hat, it doesn't mean a thing—but you're actually blushing!' He caught her by the hand. 'That's so sweet.' He kissed her lightly on the forehead. 'But I thought you told me you never blushed?'

'I did?' Merril couldn't remember telling him that.

He put a finger under her chin and looked over her face, examining it as if preparing an inventory. 'I'm sorry I barked at you just now. Sorry, eyes,' he kissed them, 'sorry, nose, ears——' then he brought his lips down and placed them on her lips '—and sorry, lips. Thank you for being so sweet. You can go home if you want to, Merril. I haven't any right to inflict this on you. It just seemed a good idea at the time.'

'I thought you said you weren't going to let me leave with my prejudices intact?'

'I think I've succeeded. Rather more than I'd hoped . . .'

Merril felt herself blushing again when she understood what he was saying, remembering the look in her own eyes in the dressing-room mirror that evening. She should have guessed he would notice and understand what that look had meant, as she had wanted him to. Now it seemed to be having the wrong effect.

'I know I'm transparent,' she muttered. 'But you wanted me to respond, didn't you? You've succeeded.' She turned away, scarcely daring to look at him, as near to offering herself to any man as she had ever been in her entire life.

'I don't want to succeed, as you put it. I'm not out to score.' Torrin let his hand drop and sat very still, just looking at her. Then after a while he reached forward and took her face between both his hands, and began to lower his lips inch by inch towards hers, as if giving her plenty of time to move away, and all this without taking his honey-gold eyes from hers. When she lifted her face up to his he touched her lips lightly and experimentally, as if unsure of her reaction.

'Are you going to slap my face?' he asked hoarsely.

Merril felt herself pressing helplessly against him as he drew her down on to the couch beside him. 'No, I don't think so,' she whispered. 'Why should I?'

'Because I'm Torrin Anthony,' he murmured, 'infamous lecher, and I've abducted you for the express purpose of having my wicked way with you, after which I shall discard you like an old sweet-paper.'

He spoke lightly, but it was so close to what she had originally thought, she dropped her glance.

'I want you,' she said simply. 'I was wrong about you. I think you're—you're absolutely marvellous.'

Her words had the same effect as a slap on the face. Torrin's hands dropped and, leaning back, he moved his head so their faces were distanced, his, at first black as thunder, adopting a professionally deadpan expression designed to give nothing away. He said, 'It's infatuation. You'll get over it when you realise I'm not wonderful. I'm vain, arrogant, selfish. I let nobody and nothing stand in the way of my ambition. Don't have any illusions about me, Merril. When I first set eyes on you, I wanted you. I wanted to take you to bed. I hadn't planned for love—I don't want it. But what I felt for you seemed so different from anything I'd felt before, I thought it was love. It was a star that beckoned and I had to follow.'

'You mean you feel differently now? You've changed?' Her eyes widened in pain. She felt as if she were falling and there was nothing to grasp on to.

'We met in very special circumstances. It made me see you as someone special. And I believe this is what happened to you, too. But I'm experienced enough to know that feelings like that can fade like snows in summer. I would never let what I feel come between

me and my work—I couldn't take that risk. Do you
understand what I'm saying?'

'I don't understand a word of it.' Only one thing
seemed clear. What he had felt had melted like
summer snow. 'When did you see me as someone
special? In your dressing-room on that first night? I
was just another backstage visitor, wasn't I? What was
so special about that? There were dozens of women
drooling over you then.' Merril was confused.

'Not then.'

'That's when we met.'

'Is it?' Torrin lay back and closed his eyes. 'I'm
exhausted. I can't think straight. Lines from the play
keep running through my head. I feel like doing
something violent.' He tried to get to his feet, having
forgotten about his fractured ankle, and groaned as he
put his weight on it. 'Damn!' His face twisted for a
moment in a look Merril knew was genuine, then he
hobbled a few paces before sitting down heavily on the
day bed again. 'Violence is obviously out. I think I'll
get some sleep instead.'

'Torrin, you can't say what you've just said to me
and then simply turn over and go to sleep!' she
exclaimed.

'You sound like an irate wife.'

'Oh, dear!' She looked down at him, his changeable
face lined with pain and the stresses of the evening's
performance, and she wanted to love him very much,
only the frightening words he had spoken to her just
now restraining her. Then she saw his yellow cat's
eyes glitter with sudden mirth at the picture of her as
an irate wife, and it made her, too, see the funny side
and she began to giggle. Without thinking, she
dropped on top of him and started to tickle him, and
suddenly he was kissing her and she was wrapped
tightly in his arms and he was crooning something in
her hair, rocking her back and forth, Merril felt tears of

relief spout from her eyes, making her bury her face in the broad shoulders against which he was tightly holding her.

'There, there,' he murmured, 'have a good cry—it's not the end of the world.' He rocked her back and forth, murmuring nothings and then saying, 'The opening of a show is always one damned crisis after another. Emotions run high. Moving into the West End doesn't happen every day, and I'm not so blasé it hasn't had its effect.' She felt him kiss the top of her head. 'None of us are thinking straight right now.'

'But, Torrin, I love you. I love you so much,' she whispered, afraid he was going to turn her away again.

He made her get up. 'Get into bed,' he ordered.

Merril slid between the silky sheets, having first made him turn away so she could finish undressing. When she gave the word, he turned back and came over to tuck her in. 'Now,' he kissed her lightly on the forehead, 'you're going to go straight to sleep. Pleasant dreams.'

'But——'

'Sleep, I said!'

'I'll only dream of you,' she warned.

'Please yourself,' he bantered, turning back to the day bed. 'Let's see how we feel about all this in the morning.'

Merril couldn't believe he was simply going to climb into a separate bed and go to sleep after he had given every impression until now that she would need an army for protection. What was going wrong? Didn't he understand that she no longer cared about the consequences? She had been wrong about her feelings to begin with, not understanding that her antagonism was a simple response to the confusion of meeting someone like him so soon after Azur.

Torrin was about to put out the light when she

called over to him. He gave a non-committal grunt and the light snapped off. She heard the rustle of covers as he made himself comfortable, then there was silence.

Merril tried to snuggle down into the capacious double bed, but it seemed desolate to be lying in it without Torrin beside her. She tossed and turned for about twenty minutes, hoping to hear him call across to her, but there was a resolute silence from the other side of the room. Unable to stand it, she slid out, feeling the thick carpet tickle her bare feet as she padded over to the day bed.

Torrin was lying on his back, one arm flung out above his head. His eyes were wide open, watching her as she stood over him.

'Torrin?'

He didn't reply.

'Torrin, you are awake, aren't you?'

'With you writhing about like a boa constrictor in a salsa contest, what do you expect?' came the curt response.

'I'm sorry——' she began.

'Never apologise. That's the first rule of good salesmanship.'

'I'm not selling anything.'

'No?' She saw his eyebrows shoot up. 'No,' he agreed then, 'you've decided to give it away, haven't you?' His voice had dropped to an ironic growl, and she had to lean forward to catch his words.

When she understood what he meant, she started back. 'That's a hateful thing to say!'

'Hateful but true. But it's my own fault. I should never have taken you backstage with me. There's something about it that makes women leave their common sense behind. It's only a job, you know, nothing special about it. But it always has the same effect. If you'd seen me heaving coal sacks about you'd probably feel quite different.'

'I doubt that.'

'Look, Merril, be a good girl and go back to bed——'

She sat down firmly on the edge of his. 'We started off on the wrong foot and now you think I'm simply stage-struck! Well, I'm not, and I want to rectify things——' She gulped a little as a panic-stricken image of what she wanted to do flooded her mind. 'I'm not very good at this sort of thing,' she went on in a hurried whisper, 'not like the scalp-hunters Tom says strew your path daily . . . I expect they're very good . . . and would know exactly what to say . . .'

As she was talking she slid her hand underneath the cover and let it ripple over the muscles of his shoulders. He gave a small groan and shifted so that she could reach further. She half expected he would try to stop her, and was daunted to find this was anything but the case.

Feeling a little out of her depth and unsure quite what she wanted, she let her instincts take over, fingers finding their own way, exploring the shield-shaped chest, circling and teasing the hard nipples, rubbing the palms of her hands rapidly over his ribs and back again to tease once more among the hairs on his chest and knead the heavier muscles across his shoulders, gratified that he seemed to find the whole thing immensely pleasurable.

Torrin moved again, making room for her beside him. 'Don't stop yet, this is heaven,' he murmured. 'You could get a job down the road any time!'

'Down the road?' she muttered, concentrating on easing away his tension and scarcely listening to his murmured words.

'Soho,' he mumbled, turning on to his stomach so that she could massage the muscles on his back. She gave him a quick nip with her teeth at the back of his neck.

'That,' she said when he protested, 'is for saying naughty things, Torrin Anthony! You know full well I would do this for no other man on earth. Not at any price.'

'Don't, Merril.' For a moment she stopped what she was doing, imagining she had hit on a painful patch, but then he went on, 'I can't let you say things like that. I'm not worth it.'

'I'll say what I like,' she murmured, adding the touch of her lips to that of her hands over the well-developed lateral muscles, kneeling over him so that her small hands could massage them equally on both sides.

'You'd better stop right now—I don't think you quite realise what you're doing to me . . .' He tried to twist his head to look up at her, but she pushed him back and continued to run her hands over his back, using more force now as she remembered movements she had learned long ago on a visit to a health farm. The masseur there had been an eighteen-stone man with shoulders like an ox, and Merril had watched, fascinated, as he exerted a rhythmic pressure over the back muscles of one of the clients. She and another reporter had volunteered to have the treatment too, and she still remembered the exquisite sensation as all the unsuspected tension had been eased away under his professional touch.

She wanted Torrin to feel like that now, so she ignored what he was saying and bent over him, using all her weight and every ounce of the skill she could muster.

He was still mumbling into his pillow and she caught odd words now and then as she worked. 'There's no future . . .' he warned. 'Don't do this . . . not think about any future . . . I want you . . . oh, you witch, that's wonderful! But right, no substance . . . coward . . . don't want commitment . . . freedom . . . won't live up to what you want . . . nothing like your dream man . . .'

'Oh, shut up, Torrin! I'm over all that now. You were quite right—I was silly to waste time mooning over someone I'm never likely to meet again, wonderful though he was. I shall always remember him, but I know it was just fantasy.' She bent to plant little kisses over his back before continuing. 'You're so beautiful,' she breathed almost to herself. 'The most beautiful man I've ever seen. Ever.'

'. . . first time like this, I hope . . . no, not fair . . . listen, I don't want responsibility for anyone else's happiness . . . enough problems . . . don't want commitment . . .' He half turned his head. 'Are you listening, Merril?'

'Of course I am, Torrin darling—or should I say Tory darling?' she whispered against his ear. 'Does your brunette friend do this sort of thing for you?' she went on, nibbling the lobe of his ear and feeling suddenly very sophisticated and grown-up about love.

'Merril, listen to me. You were right, I'm the sort who runs away . . . haven't the courage to stay . . . takes real courage to live up to that daily commitment to someone else. I don't have courage like that . . .'

'Never mind.' Merril wasn't really listening. 'Is that nice?' she murmured, sliding her hands down in smooth swooshing movements from shoulder to waist.

'Nearly nice.'

'What's wrong with it, my darling?'

'Stops too soon——' he mumbled again, turning back to bury his head in the pillow and groaning as she took him at his word and let her hands pressure further, moving down in a V from the apex of his shoulders to the narrow waist until, greatly daring, she could feel the hard muscles of his buttocks beneath her palms, then she was bringing her hands

down again and again until she could scarcely tell the
difference between his body and her own. Suddenly
he gave a groan and twisted over in one abrupt
movement, grasping hold of both her hands to rake
them roughly down the length of his body, drawing
her down on top of him at the same time in one
powerful movement.

Merril gave a cry as she discovered why he had
been trying to warn her to stop, and at the same time
felt his hands slide round her hips, dragging her
against him so that she was straddled helplessly
across him, her automatic protests dying at once as
she felt him lock her against his body. In the darkness
she could only make out the pale blur of his face
against the pillow, unable to see his expression, and
she put out a hand to explore his face.

'You can't drive a man wild . . .' he licked her
fingers, catching them in his lips and kissing the palm
of her hand as it fluttered over his mouth' . . .
without taking the consequences. You know that,
don't you, angel?'

'I love you, Torrin.'

Putting a finger over her lips, he muttered further
feverish endearments, drawing her down and down
over him so that she felt as helpless as a rag doll, all
resistance turned to yearning as his strength
transported her to a heaven she had never dreamed
of, all words but the one that was his name scoured
from her mind in the ecstasy of the moment.

She lay collapsed across him, one of his arms
heavily resting across her back to stop her slipping off
the narrow day bed, his own head thrown back
across the pillows. His lips pressured gently against
the side of her neck as she moved up to kiss him.
'We're an impractical pair,' he murmured after a
while, 'there's a perfectly sound double bed across
the room . . . Come on,' he urged, forgetting his

fractured ankle and cursing under his breath as he put pressure on it again.

Merril slithered into the cold sheets beside him. 'This is heaven, Torrin! I never knew it could be like this. It must be the best kept secret in the world.'

'Idiot, I don't know where you've been living! Come here, that was only a beginning . . .' Injury forgotten, he began to give her a lesson in love she knew she would never forget.

It was early next morning while they were both still sleeping that Tom rang, as promised, to tell Torrin he'd fixed an appointment with Wardrobe. 'How are you feeling, love?' she heard him ask.

'Not bad,' replied Torrin.

Merril lowered her lashes. Not bad? She felt wonderful. She imagined how she would scold Torrin when he came off the phone for being so grudging about such a wonderful night. Then another thougth popped unbidden into her head— some comment about stage-struck women—and she had a nightmare picture of this being the sort of thing to happen to him all the time. The thought was so horrible, she prayed it wasn't true. She jerked her head round to watch him when he replaced the receiver, as if she would be able to read his past in his face.

'She's going to come up here to take measurements, so we needn't get up just yet,' he remarked, oblivious to the turmoil of her thoughts.

She allowed him to put his arms around her and they lay in each other's arms until the very last minute when Torrin finally had to reach out to ring down for breakfast. He wouldn't let her get dressed, and she hid under the blankets as the trolley was wheeled in.

'Hotels are one of the last places in which one can

justify having breakfast in bed,' he told her sternly. 'No hotel manager worth his salt feels he's doing a proper job if his guests leap forth at crack of dawn to vacate their rooms without first having dined like Caesar recumbent.'

'As an argument it's rather poor, but I'm too comfortable to argue,' Merril replied, propping herself up against him when the waiter had left and nibbling on a piece of cinnamon toast.

'Do you do this sort of thing often?' she ventured at last in a small voice, trying to sound casual and half hoping he might think she simply meant having breakfast in bed in hotels; but it was too much like the question she had asked the previous night and he obviously took it as a direct probe into other affairs.

'Don't probe! It lacks style.'

'Sor——' she began, then snapped her mouth shut. 'No, I meant breakfast in bed,' she muttered, suddenly chilled by the deliberate intrusion of the outside world and the inference to be drawn from Torrin's reticence.

'Hotel breakfasts in bed? Whenever I can. One needs some comfort during a tour. It can be hell moving from town to town all the time.' He settled back. 'I used to tour six months of the year with a small theatre company, everyone mucking in with the loading of the props, setting up and so on—even driving the truck from venue to venue. That was soon after I left drama school. Wonderful years, but damned hard work, and one certainly learns to search out the little luxuries that make life bearable.'

'Like some friendly girl in your bed, I suppose?' Merril couldn't help remarking.

He laughed and gave her a little hug, but didn't agree or disagree. She was thoughtful as they break-fasted, becoming increasingly aware that, despite their lovemaking, Torrin's attitude to her had changed in a subtle way. It had really begun since their argument at the mill, only being made worse when he got hold of the idea that she was stage-struck. She tried to recall what it was she had said during their argument that had seemed to trigger off his change, but could only muster a hazy recollection of that stormy scene.

Last night his own warning had been clear enough, but she had chosen to ignore it, not really believing he could mean it, and, in the ecstasy of loving him, feeling herself invincible—powerful enough to make him love her by the sheer force of her own desire.

Now, in the light of day, things were not so cut and dried. Torrin himself was not the unresisting force he had been then.

Merril burned to get things straight, but was frightened to hear his reply until, at the very last moment, just as he was levering himself over the side of the bed, she said tersely, 'Am I just a one-night stand to you, Torrin? Tell me.' He dropped back heavily on the edge and put his head in his hands, his face concealed, and for a moment or two didn't bother to reply. Then he turned to her. His face was wiped of all expression again. 'I warned you you'd got it right from the very beginning. I'm not a hero, I'm made of flesh and blood. And I'm open to temptation, as you've seen. I'm not your dream lover, Merril.'

'I don't expect that any more. It was unrealistic,' she said miserably.

'I warned you not to expect anything from me in the way of commitment. Don't let's have regrets now when it's too late.'

He turned round to look at her. She was sitting bolt upright, blonde hair tousled from the touch of his own hands, face flushed after a night's lovemaking, her breasts, uncovered, glowing with a pearly lustre.

He looked at her for a long time without moving, then gave a flip smile. 'One-night stand?' A muscle worked at the side of his jaw. 'No, I don't see you like that.'

He turned away, but when he turned back there was a crooked smile on his face as he caught her eyes. 'One night isn't enough. You've still a lot to learn. Two or three might cover the curriculum, though.'

She could see he wanted to keep things light, but his reply tore her apart. She had been right to be wary, knowing all along this would happen. Torrin was simply too spoiled by constant admiration to take her seriously. He hadn't understood how much it had cost her to surrender to him. It was more than she had ever given any man in her life. And now he was telling her it was over.

'No regrets,' she replied bravely. 'I might even sign on for another course of lessons. I'll let you know.'

Unable to keep up the don't-care manner a moment longer, she leaped out of bed and made a pretence of racing to the bathroom first, jeering at him through the door as he limped after her. Pretending it was all a game, she slammed the door and locked it. Then she switched the shower full on to drown out the sound of the sobs that wrenched through her.

CHAPTER EIGHT

THE GIRL from Wardrobe and her assistant had already arrived by the time Merril emerged from the shower, flushed, and not a little embarrassed at the thoughts that would be going through their heads when they saw her with only a bath towel draped around her. With a muttered greeting she snatched up her clothes and retreated into the privacy of the bathroom once more to put them on.

Their task was finished by the time she re-emerged. This time she had made up her face and done her hair, and hoped she was looking more self-possessed than she felt. The wardrobe mistress, Marie, was sitting on the floor, resting her head against Torrin's 'good' leg, and they were chatting in a friendly, intimate manner that made Merril purse her lips. She knew it was silly to feel jealous, but she did, she couldn't help it. Especially when Marie turned to him and in response to something Torrin said, smiled up wickedly and announced, 'I know your measurements as well as I know my own, darling, so don't fret.'

'What did she mean by that?' exclaimed Merril as soon as the door closed behind the two girls.

He looked puzzled.

'Oh, never mind, Tory darling,' she whipped back, then regretted showing her feelings so plainly when she saw the bored look on his face as he understood what she was getting at.

'You can opt out any time you like, Merril.' He shrugged his shoulders into his jacket, still sitting down to save his ankle, and when she didn't answer he said, 'OK—so do we go or don't we?'

She felt her breath stop. Now was the point of no return. She gave a brief nod.

On the way down she avoided his glance, helping unobtrusively by holding open the lift doors and wondering if they would have time to unravel the knot of misunderstanding between them before they parted. Thinking ahead to that time, she asked, 'When do you *want* me to leave?'

Torrin's reply was interrupted by the arrival of the black Jaguar. It stopped as close to the hotel doors as possible and the chauffeur came up the steps, holding out an arm for Torrin. Evidently someone had kept him up to date with the situation. Merril wondered what it cost to employ someone like that, plus car, plus parkside mansion . . . Somehow it didn't make sense, unless Torrin had appeared in films and made his money that way. He would never have toured for so long in the conditions he had described earlier if his family were as well-heeled as she had first imagined.

When they were settled in the car and it was speeding down the Strand, she asked him again. 'When do you want me to leave?'

'I heard you the first time, and I'm still thinking about it.' His eyes narrowed. 'What about you? When do *you* want to leave?'

Never, Merril thought, averting her face. 'I can come back to town tonight,' she muttered eventually. 'Whenever it suits you.'

'Tomorrow morning would suit me better,' he replied at once.

So be it, she thought. It was a slight reprieve. At least she had given him the option of getting rid of her sooner. But then, after last night, why should he? The cynicism of her attitude was untypical, but she couldn't help it. Last night she had simply provided a little of the 'luxury' he had learned to seek out, hadn't she? The thought brought a tear of humiliation to the corners of her eyes. Her pride was in shreds, but she couldn't bring herself to leave him until he asked her to go. She would stay as long as possible. Every minute would be counted and stored and afterwards preserved in the archives of her memory as something special and unrepeatable.

As before, the driver dropped them in the grove and they walked back over the wooden bridge towards the house. The millstream was still swollen after the previous day's rainstorm, and Merril shuddered as she looked down into the powerful current. Torrin had saved her life. As they paused on the bridge she touched his arm but found herself unable to frame the words that would tell him of the depth of her emotion. He seemed to understand what was making her tongue-tied, for after glancing down at the rushing water he tightened his grip on her arm before giving a little shrug, a slight smile softening the austerity of his expression. 'Close shave, hm?' He pushed her on ahead, limping slightly as he followed her into the garden.

After lunch which was waiting for them, prepared, he explained, by a woman from the village who had also brought in the Sunday papers, Torrin settled down before the log fire blazing cheerfully in the open fireplace and with his foot resting on a stool began to go through the contents of a leather bag he had brought back from the theatre.

'Anything I can do to help?' asked Merril, coming to sit next to him.

'Stopped taking notes, have you?' he teased, looking human all of a sudden.

'I made all the notes I wanted last night,' she retorted drily. 'What are you doing now?'

'My usual Sunday morning task, a little late this weekend.' He pushed some letters over to her. It was fan mail, she saw that at once, much of it written on lurid-coloured notepaper, some of it scented, she noticed with a faint smile. Teenage girls. She had never gone through that phase, not having had much interest in pop idols or film stars at that age herself.

'Do you always get this much?' she asked.

'There's a little more this week, with the opening.' He gave a chuckle. 'Read this, she sounds priceless!'

Merril blushed as she read the impassioned declarations scrawled in a large schoolgirl hand on pink notepaper. 'Honestly!' She hastily put it with the others. 'How on earth do you answer that sort of thing?'

'Mainly I hand the lot over to my agent. One of the secretaries sees that they get answered once I've looked them over. Some of them are rather sweet,' he paused, 'others not.'

Before she could ask what he meant a photograph of a very pretty girl of about seventeen fell out of one of the envelopes. Torrin eyed it appreciatively, and his expression made Merril turn away. She got up rather hurriedly and went to refill their coffee-cups from the pot in the hearth. When she turned round he was already opening the next one. No wonder he looked as if he had heard it all before when she said she loved him! she thought. Her declaration had been pale stuff compared to these purple pages. But her love was real, wasn't it? These—these others, they were just teenage dreams.

She came to sit on the floor at his feet. 'Torrin, how will you ever believe a woman really loves you after being brainwashed by all these fantastic, ephemeral protestations?'

'Not so ephemeral, some of them,' he replied, continuing to read a long letter, several pages of it, until, reaching the end, he said, 'This particular girl has been writing to me for the last eighteen months. Saw me in some production up north.'

'Why? Why does she do it?'

'Life unsatisfactory, perhaps? She has two small children, an unimaginative husband and an ageing, incontinent father to look after with no hope of anything better for a very long time. I'm her little bit of escapism, her dream lover who keeps her sane in an impossible situation. And why not?'

'It's ridiculous! Don't they realise what fools they're making of themselves?'

He shook his head. 'Life's been good to you. You can't possibly imagine what it's like to be trapped in a situation you don't want but which for various reasons you're forced to endure—courage makes them go on, they should be admired, not mocked. I would run away if things weren't to my liking. So, too, in all probability, would you. But some of these women, they go on and on, caring for their families, struggling to make ends meet, surviving under impossible conditions. They're the salt of the earth.'

His voice, his words, even the phrases he was using, reminded Merril of what Azur had said about the villagers he took her to meet, the ones caught up in a war they didn't want. It made her gasp. 'Have you——' She broke off. Of course he hadn't said these things before, yet it gave her such a sense of *déjà vu*, she was thrown into confusion.

'What's the matter?' Torrin noticed her change of colour.

'Nothing,' she replied, her heart fluttering before she could bring it under control. Then, pulling herself together, she asked, 'Are you right? Is it courage? Or is it stupidity that makes people go on heedlessly, mindlessly, year after year?' An image of her mother flashed before her eyes, her mother waiting by the phone for news of her war correspondent husband in

one trouble spot or another. Her mother never missing
the news in case there was something about the latest
foreign war. She had scarcely had enough peace of
mind to live a life of her own. Merril had despised her
for it.

'Wouldn't it be better if they got up and did something about the situation they're in, if it's so hard to
endure?' She felt a flush of anger lash her face as she
fought against some deep-seated response. 'I would
fight back! I wouldn't lapse into day-dreams—I'd *do*
something! I couldn't bear not to change things.'

'And if things couldn't be changed?'

'Then I'd die in the attempt!' She broke off again as
something struck her with unpleasant clarity. In a
minor way wasn't she herself simply lapsing into a
dream of what-might-have-been? First over Azur, and
now over Torrin himself? For instead of standing up
and telling him he could go to hell, she was passively
enduring the agony of knowing she meant nothing to
him, and suffering it because she felt compelled to, by
love in her case. And it wasn't duty, or any of those
other reasons some of these women had for putting up
with lives devoid of hope, but love, some would say a
self-chosen torment.

What made it easier still, she knew it would be over
tomorrow. Compared to long years of endurance, it
needed little courage to get through one day of hell.

Her eyes glistened. 'I should show more sympathy,'
she muttered. 'I'm——' She smiled bitterly. 'If I was
allowed to say I'm sorry, I would do.'

'Good—well, don't. It's enough to feel it.' Torrin put
his head on one side. 'Don't look so miserable
—they're not all sob stories. Some of them are fun,
they're simply looking for a little spice. They can be
very naughty indeed!'

'Do you ever meet any of them?' she asked. 'I mean,
after they've written to you?'

'Sometimes. They turn up at the stage door expecting me to remember everything they told me about themselves.'

'What do you do?'

'It depends.'

'On what?'

'On what they want,' he shrugged.

'Would you give them what they want?'

'Sex, you mean?' he asked brutally.

Merril nodded, averting her head.

He didn't answer straight away and she turned back to gauge his expression. He was smiling.

'Well?' she demanded more sharply than she intended.

'Of course I don't. It'd be very one-sided, wouldn't it? I'd be taking advantage of them.'

'You took advantage of me last night!' she flared back before she could stop herself.

'On the contrary, you took advantage of *me* . . .' His expression was amused.

'I——?' Her mouth opened in astonishment.

'That was the last thing on my mind last night, and I warned you what would happen if you went on seducing me in that wanton fashion, but you were determined to ignore my warnings, weren't you? I had no choice once you'd got me to the point of no return.' Torrin was chuckling softly now and, putting out a hand, began to smooth the hair back from her crimsoning face. 'I was utterly helpless—it was a wonderful, a unique experience——'

'You didn't say it was wonderful this morning on the phone to Tom,' Merril observed suspiciously, sure he was acting again, and embarrassed beyond belief at the image he apparently now had of her.

'You don't imagine I'm going to tell Tom about my sex life, do you? It'd be all round the theatre in five minutes.'

'I thought he knew everything about it already?'

'He thinks he does.'

He leaned forward and dragged her towards him. 'I can't move about much because of this damned ankle. Be nice to me. Make it easy.'

Merril shuddered. His eyes were like lightning, alive, full of shock and energy. She could feel herself sinking out of reach of common sense again under their power. It was a drowning feeling. But this was why she had agreed to come back to the millhouse, wasn't it? He had told her she could opt out earlier that morning and she had wilfully pushed her qualms aside. She reached out, slipping her arms around his neck, accepting the consequences.

'At least you're not disobeying doctor's orders,' she murmured, hiding her face against his neck so he couldn't see the anguish in her eyes. 'He told you not to go flying. Was he serious?'

'I usually take a plane up on Sundays. There's an airfield just down the road,' mumbled Torrin, intent on pulling her blouse open.

'When did you learn?' she asked, clinging on to the question as if to keep talking would save her from the swooning of her senses as his hands cupped her breasts.

'At school,' he mumbled, dipping his head. 'I'll teach you, if you like.'

'Me?' She felt white heat flood over her at his touch. He bent to press his lips against her breasts, then raised his head, eyes raking over her flushed face.

'I can just imagine you in a flying suit and white Biggles scarf with all these blonde tendrils escaping from your helmet, piloting in with the latest news,' he told her, moving his hands down over her back as he brought himself up against her.

By now the buttons of his shirt were undone, and

as if by magic her skirt and panties had come right off. She felt him pressing her down on to the fur rug in front of the fire and his lips began to brush a tantalising pathway between her breasts, forcing a little groan of pleasure through her lips, then he was driving her feelings to fever pitch with a magical choreography of touch that left her breathless.

It was evening by the time they got around to looking at the papers. 'I haven't even read my reviews,' observed Torrin, hooking one arm round Merril's shoulders while he tried to lever himself up to open the pages with one hand. They were still lying on the fur rug by the fire. 'You hold a corner,' he said, butting the edge of the paper with his head. 'This is too perfect a position to change just yet.'

'Maybe we should get dressed?' Merril suggested, holding one side of the paper so they could read it together.

'Tomorrow morning'll do,' he mumbled, eyes scanning a column closest to him. 'Hey, so I was right!' he exclaimed after a moment. 'Why did you deny it?'

'What?'

'You're nominated for the young journalist of the year award.'

'I am?'

'If your name's Merril Park. Is it?' he asked, narrowing his eyes at her.

Even though it was a joke, she tormented herself with the thought that he must forget some of the names some time. She read the same small paragraph. 'It's true!' she exclaimed. 'Ray must have known even when he was telling me off the other day, the devil. I'll never trust him again!'

'Should know better than to trust media people,' Torrin remarked, and as she bared her teeth at him he said, 'Sorry!' earning a little nip of reproof before she kissed him better.

It was breaking her heart to play like this, but at least his memories of her would be good ones, and her pride would never let him know how much he was hurting.

'Dad would have been pleased I'm being nominated, even though I don't suppose I'll win,' she observed with a twinge of sadness that her father hadn't lived to see how well she was doing.

'What about your mother?'

'What about her?' Her lip curled.

'Won't she be pleased?'

'Not particularly. She never wanted me to be a journalist. She's the type who would prefer me to have a nice boring husband and lots of babies.'

'Mothers do, so I've heard. And why not? What's wrong with babies? I quite like 'em.'

'Other people's, no doubt,' Merril responded tartly. 'Well, I'm not giving up my career to be trapped in a house with a lot of howling kiddies!'

'It isn't a question of "either/or" these days, though. Lots of women seem to combine a career, a boring husband *and* a houseful of offspring without any trouble,' he observed mildly.

'That's not what you were saying yesterday in your study,' she retorted, examining his face to see if it gave anything away. It didn't.

'Yesterday?'

'Don't pretend you don't remember. You were unbelievable.'

'Oh, that wasn't me, that was Ron Smith. A TV part I turned down the other day,' Torrin explained with a disarming grin.

'So you were acting?'

'Couldn't you tell?'

'I never can.'

'No . . .' his eyes licked over her face '. . . I do believe you mean it.'

'Don't, Torrin!' she begged.

'Don't what?' His voice had dropped several intervals, sending shivers down her spine.

'Don't—don't look at me like that . . .'

'I can't help the way I look at you. You take my breath away. You look so beautiful, beautiful and wanton . . . naked as nature intended——' He tried to lighten the suddenly serious mood that had got them in its grip, but it fell flat, and as if pulled together by some invisible force they came together in a burning collision of mutual desire.

I know he's only playing a role, cried Merril inwardly, but it will have to be enough. Tomorrow's heartache isn't far away. The masquerade is nearly over. And she closed her eyes, giving herself to Torrin's loving touch without restraint.

The rest of the time spent at the millhouse, living up to her image of it as a secret love-nest, made Merril feel as if she was cocooned in a fairy-tale world of love. As long as she could ignore the future, it was paradise enough to lie awake in Torrin's arms, forcing sleep away so she wouldn't miss a single precious moment of their last hours together.

She could hear the cascading of the water through the sluice as it fell from the silent depths of the millpool to the narrow cut that would take it tumbling down the hillside to the river in the valley, and later, much changed, to join the sea, and she felt her love was like that, rising from a deep source within her, then pitching headlong, turbulently, joyfully, inevitably, to become as limitless and enduring as the ocean itself.

It seemed impossible for love like that to come to an end. She could not believe as the hours of the night unfolded that, come morning, she and Torrin would part for ever. Yet she would have to watch him say goodbye—their two or three nights of love complete.

The Jaguar pulled into the side of the road, straddling the double yellow lines outside the office with lordly defiance of the regulations, and Torrin was the first to come to life, sliding across the leather seat to open the door for her and climbing out on to the pavement to help her out.

Breakfast at the millhouse had been a silent affair. Merril, determined to walk away with her head held high, with a show of style Torrin would respect, had been unable to pretend to the extent of carrying on lighthearted chit-chat over the muesli. Not when her heart was lying in a thousand pieces at her feet. Engulfed in misery, she could only go through the motions, answering when spoken to, reserving her comments for practicalities, desperate to see some sign that he had changed his mind. But there was no sign. What he said, he meant. She had chosen to give herself to him and now she had to face the consequences.

He was taking his time about climbing back into the car. The journey had passed in almost total silence. It had seemed as if he was waiting for Merril to break down, plead with him perhaps to let her stay, but pride would not let her give him that satisfaction.

He was looking at his watch. 'You're early. What about coffee before you go in?'

'You don't drink coffee,' she reminded him.

Torrin was about to say something, then stopped. His shoulders braced and he dug both hands in his jacket pockets. 'Thanks for looking after me this weekend. I hope the article writes itself. And—er—good luck with the award. I'll be keeping my fingers crossed for you.'

He sounded like someone reciting a rather boring speech rehearsed too often.

'Thank you.' Merril looked up at the glass box into which she would soon have to disappear. There didn't seem much left to say. 'I hope I don't misrepresent you.' She tried to smile, but it felt like a grimace. She dashed a hand across her eyes.

'All right?' He bent his head, but she shied back.

'It's nothing—some dust. It's gone now.' She blinked once or twice. 'Well, that's that, then. Thank you for your time,' she said stiltedly. She wondered if it was always like this for Torrin the morning after. He playing it cool, trying to make things easy, the girl dashing away tears, on the verge of breaking down. He must be able to see how she felt.

Unable to bear it any longer, she swivelled suddenly and, without looking back, ran up the shallow steps into the building before he could call out.

'Had a good rest, sweetheart? I must say you're looking blooming!' It was Mike, Merril's rival at the next desk. She had spent twenty minutes in the Ladies erasing all traces of emotion from her face.

'I feel terrific, thanks,' she lied. 'I've been working, actually.'

'Oh, yes?' Mike's glance narrowed.

'Relax, it wouldn't interest you. I was doing that piece on Torrin Anthony. Didn't anybody mention it?'

'Only each of the secretaries, singly and at great length, including the married ones, but apart from them, no . . . Except for every other woman in the building,' Mike added as an afterthought. There was a suggestive glint in his eyes when he asked, 'Does he live up to his reputation, then? Bet you didn't have much time to make notes!'

She smiled, extending a hand to tap her notebook. 'It's all here, Mike. And I'm just wondering how much I'd get for it from our rivals down the road.' Then she remembered with stark precision just what Torrin's own rider to that remark had been, and she bit her lip, swinging forward in her seat as if she'd got plenty to be getting on with.

Luckily, Mike was busy and she could return to her secret misery under a pretence of filing a report.

The day seemed to drag. By the time she managed to leave, superstitiously avoiding the place where their goodbye had taken place, the lights along the street were already coming on. Merril headed for Charing Cross tube, forcing herself to pass the theatre with his name emblazoned all over the front, but not daring to let her glance slither along the side of the theatre to the stage door.

It took her mind off Torrin to have to fight her way through the rush-hour crowds, and when she finally reached the flat she burst in with a hello to Annie that sounded cheerful enough to fool the most astute listener.

'So, aren't you the lucky one!' Annie, beaming, came straight through from the kitchen, a big blue and white apron tied around her middle, long red hair fastened back in a scarf knotted at her nape.

'Lucky?' Supposing she was referring to the weekend, Merril tried to give a smile, but Annie was already pointing to an enormous bouquet of flowers lying on the sitting-room table.

'Need I ask what took place? Would I be so tactless!' She bustled back as a smell of burning wafted through the open door. 'They were outside when I got in from work,' she called over her shouder. 'There's a card underneath.'

Hands shaking, Merril lifted the flowers and opened the envelope that was there. 'To Merril,' she read. 'From Torrin.' That was it. No greeting. Well, what had she expected? It was a gracious thank-you to one of life's little luxuries.

Unable to stop herself, she felt her face begin to

crumple, then sobs were racking through her body, and somehow Annie was holding her and bit by bit the whole story was tumbling out as between sobs Merril tried to explain what she didn't yet understand herself. 'How could I be so *stupid*?' she sobbed. 'I've behaved like a complete idiot, but I just couldn't—I couldn't help it,' she cried. 'I don't know what came over me. I *knew* what I was doing. He warned me. He said, don't— don't expect anything . . .'

'He's a bastard. He's not worth a single, solitary tear. Men like him deserve to be shot. You'll see that when you've had a good cry.' Annie proffered a box of Kleenex and, seeing that Merril was incapable of drying her own tears yet, dabbed randomly at her face, murmuring, 'You'll feel better soon, love. It'll soon be over.'

Merril let Annie make her a cup of tea, sipping it and giving her a shamefaced look that expressed what she felt now. 'I must have been suffering from some form of madness,' she said at last. 'He didn't make me any promises. At first, you see, it was different. He seemed—well, I suppose he simply tried to get me into bed in a sort of straightforward manner. I didn't really believe he meant it when he started to say he loved me.'

She stopped. 'Obviously I didn't believe it. Even though he would have seemed pretty plausible if I hadn't kept remembering he was an actor. I was feeling—well, something pretty wild, too. I mean—hell, Annie, he is gorgeous.' She bit back the tears and tried to arrange her feelings so that they made sense.

'We had a sort of argument. I suppose he was annoyed that I was holding out against him. I don't know—it's all a bit of a haze. And then I remember running away from him into the garden——'

'The beast! He scared you that much?'

'No. Oh, I don't know. I thought I'd show him. I thought I'd get away—I was just scared, I knew I was going to give in—guessing even then what would happen if I did. I kept trying to tell myself he didn't live up to my ideal, but it's as if I didn't really look at him properly until too late. I made myself keep thinking of Azur instead. I even taunted him a bit——' Merril bit her lip.

'And it made him mad?'

She nodded.

'So then he threatened to show you what a real man was like?'

She nodded again. 'Something like that. But not so obvious . . .'

'What happened when you ran outside?'

'I nearly drowned. I fell into his damned millrace.'

'Millrace?' Annie opened her eyes.

So Merril told her all about the house and the chauffeur-driven Jaguar and the mansion in the park.

'Gee! He's not some sort of drug merchant, is he? It costs, property like that. A Jag, for heaven's sake! Are you sure it didn't belong to the theatre?'

'No. It seemed to come with the mansion.'

Annie gave her a sympathetic hug. 'If you're going to lose your head and your heart, you may as well do it in style! But, Merril, you'll get over him, really you will. Tell me,' she interrupted herself, 'what happened when you fell in the millrace? Did he turn out to be a wimp? Did you have to drag yourself out, covered in weed?'

'Not at all. He was fantastic. I must have knocked my head on a rock or something, because I passed out, and when I came round I was lying in his arms in the grass on the riverbank further down. He was soaked, so I guess he'd had to dive in after me. He also fractured his ankle and went on stage that night without a murmur, not telling anyone till after the show. It must have been excruciating for him.'

'The show must go on.'

'Exactly.' Merril ignored Annie's ironic tone. 'The

theatre doctor thought he needed locking up, by the
look on his face. So did his dresser, Tommy. And, I
suppose, so did I. It was the way he was then as much
as anything that made me realise I'd been so wrong
about him. It was the sort of thing Azur would have
done, maybe, or Dad.'

'Or Superman. That's the type you really go for,
isn't it?' remarked Annie.

Merril ignored the hint of criticism. 'We had to stay
in town overnight, so we went to a hotel, and it was
then I did the most stupid thing in my entire life—I
seduced him.'

'*You* seduced *him*?'

'I know. It seems unbelievable now.'

'Oh, Merril, you mean you let him persuade you
into thinking you were making the running?'

'No, it wasn't like that at all. I really was,' she
admitted, shamefaced again.

'And he just lay back and let it happen? After
making such a play for you at the beginning?'

'By this time he seemed to have decided that he
didn't want to know,' Merril mumbled.

'Neat technique. I wonder if it always works?' Annie
looked contrite. 'Sorry, darling, I'm just an old cynic.
Take no notice. But it does seem unlikely he'd be
totally indifferent to you.' She gave Merril's vivacious
blonde beauty an appraising look, noticing with the
detached vision of a fashion writer that she really did
have the looks men went mad for, and shook her head
wonderingly. 'Are you sure you haven't misunderstood him? Did he seriously tell you it was all over
between you?' She glanced at the mass of long-
stemmed roses.

Merril's lips set in a firm line and she could only
nod. She took another sip of tea, by now cold, but she
scarcely noticed. When she felt braver she said the
words engraved on her heart. 'He said, ''I'm not your

dream lover—I'm flesh and blood. I'm open to temptation like any other man. I don't want commitment. I'm a coward—you were right.'' And it's true, Annie. He meant every word.'

'So he sends you flowers? Red roses, note.'

'It's just his style.'

'Style? To go around breaking hearts?' Annie got up. 'You could have any man in town and you go and choose a cold, conniving beast like that? Darling, I'll give you two days to get over this little heartbreak, then I'm going to take you in hand. I'm not having one of the most gorgeous friends I possess pining away over a worthless, arrogant man who hasn't the brain to recognise a good woman when she throws herself into his bed. Be warned—this is war!'

Merril was grateful for Annie's no-nonsense approach, even though she didn't for a minute go along with it. Torrin wasn't any of those things Annie said, it just looked like that because she hadn't been able to explain properly what he was really like. How could she, when, as Tommy had told her, he was an original?

CHAPTER NINE

ANNIE soon guessed that something was wrong, and when there was no more mention of Torrin Anthony, she did everything she could to draw Merril into her circle of cocktail parties, dinners and weekends in the country. She even persuaded her to attend a summer ball, though it wasn't Merril's scene, and she introduced her to so many eligibles that Merril felt dazed to think that London was crammed with such numbers of wife-hunting young men. But the Nigels and the Hughs, the Frazers and the Richards passed like a distant procession, and Merril was scarcely aware of the hands she shook, the hands, in the back of taxis, she avoided, with a polite, distancing smile never leaving her face. She heard herself referred to as 'an ice maiden' and felt only a little guilt that she was throwing Annie's generous attempt to help her through a rough patch back in her face.

'I really have an article to finish,' she began to apologise more frequently when Annie suggested some entertainment or other, and in fact she began to work increasingly hard, taking on extra shifts whenever she could, and using her spare evenings to build up some freelance work with a group of women's magazines.

Every day as it dragged by seemed like a month, and that first month seemed like a decade. In all that time she would take the long way to the tube on her journeys to and from work to avoid passing Torrin's theatre. One evening it was raining heavily as she came out of the office and, believing she must be over the worst of him, she decided to risk the shorter route, putting her head down and bravely marching in the direction of the Strand.

Rush-hour traffic crawled and snarled along beside her as she approached the theatre. As she drew level she braced herself, intending to permit herself a quick glance into the glass showcase on the wall outside where Torrin's photograph would be enshrined. But when she drew level she couldn't help stopping.

His image was engraved so deeply into her memory, it was a shock to see the black and white studio photograph, with the familiar face smiling down at her just as she remembered it. Rain was sweeping in great gusts into the portico of the theatre but, ignoring it, Merril went right up to the case and peered in. As soon as she allowed her glance to dwell on that familiar smile, tears began to trickle down her cheeks before she could stop them, and as if in sympathy rain started to streak the front of the glass. She stood for an age watching the drops slowly obliterate Torrin's face behind a watery screen.

'Hello, lovely, you're quite a stranger round here!' A nearby voice broke into her reverie and she swivelled in surprise at being addressed, then gave a start as she recognised the figure standing beside her. It was Tom, fake fur bedraggled by the rain, his collar pulled right up for protection.

'Rather damp out here. Fancy popping backstage for a cup of coffee and a chat?'

'No!' she yelped, stepping back. 'I mean—it's nice to see you, Tom, but I haven't time to stop.' She looked hurriedly at her watch, wondering if the gesture seemed convincing.

He gave her a friendly smile. 'You'd be extremely welcome, you know.'

'I can't. I really can't——' She half turned. It was sweet of him to say these things, but she remembered what Torrin himself had said about not believing a word Tom told her. She could imagine how embarrassing it would be if Torrin should accidentally walk in and see her sitting there in his dressing-room, chatting to Tom. What on earth would they say to each other? It was something too unbearable to contemplate.

'Must go,' she said hurriedly.

'Take care, sweetheart. We think of you.'

With a gasp Merril plunged off along the pavement. When she turned to look back, Tom was still standing in the portico with the collar of his fake fur tilted against the rain, gazing after her with an expression she was too upset to recognise.

After that there was the awards ceremony.

'Cornel and I are organising a team of supporters. If you win we'll go wild at that new nightclub in Covent Garden. And if you lose—we'll do exactly the same, though with slightly longer faces. Now, what are you going to wear?'

'What?' Merril had scarcely looked up from the article she was rewriting for the hundredth time. The piece about Torrin had gone out long ago, and now she was working on a piece about health farms. The drawback was that an image of a broad, muscular back sliding silkily beneath her hands would keep coming into her head, spoiling her concentration.

She ripped another piece of paper out of the typewriter and turned. 'You're simply ruining my concentration, Annie!' she complained in the sort of tones Tom would have used. Then she gave a wan smile to see Annie's expression. 'Why do I need to dress up? The chaps won't. I shall go as I am.'

'You will not! And if you think they're all going to turn up in baggy cords with leather patches on their elbows, or battle-stained jeans as per usual, think again. You'll have some stiff competition, fashion-wise, and you're not letting us down.'

'I think your priorities are all wrong.'

'Right. All image and no substance. Now, don't be earnest. What have you got?' demanded Annie.

'To wear, you mean? You look. I'd be happy in a sack.'

'I think a trip round the boutiques is on,' reported Annie when she returned from rummaging around in Merril's cupboards. She looked pleased at the prospect.

'I'm glad I'm not put up for one of these awards every day,' grumbled Merril later, after they'd trekked round Annie's favourite shops, bought two complete outfits with hefty discounts, as Annie was known, and finally staggered back to the flat with arms laden and feet aching.

'I might do a feature on you, darling. ''What to wear for that award-winning dinner''—would you model for me?'

'Will you pay me?' asked Merril unexpectedly.

'You're surprisingly mercenary these days. What are you doing with all this cash you're earning?' It was spoken lightly, but when Merril blushed Annie stopped in her tracks. 'Heavens, what have I said? Is anything wrong?'

'Not at all. But you're quite right—I'm not spending it. I'm saving. I've decided to resign from my job and go back to look for Azur.' Merril gave Annie a baleful stare. 'The paper's too damned mean to send me back, so I'm going to get the fare myself. Azur is the one man in the world who's worth chasing. I'm sick of the Torrin Anthony type. I remember saying to him once that if I was in a hopeless situation I wouldn't put up with it. I'd get out, or die in the attempt. Well, that's what I'm doing now—I'm getting out.'

'To me, it looks like running away,' observed Annie

caustically as she recovered from this outburst.

'I'm not running——'

'But,' insisted Annie, 'I think you are. I think you're too scared to face up to a little bit of heartbreak. You're running from reality.'

Merril tightened her lips. 'If this is reality, you can keep it!'

Observing her obstinate expression, Annie diplomatically let the matter drop. Merril's outburst put a blight on the performance of trying on new clothes. She couldn't hide what she thought about Merril's intention, and Merril was adamant that she wasn't going to stay in London another week longer than necessary.

'Soon I shall have enough money to go, especially if they take the article I'm working on now,' she explained after the clothes had been hung up out of the way. 'I know what I'm doing. I'll have enough put by to live for some time out there. The cost of living's very low and I have few personal needs. It's for the best, Annie, you'll see.'

'Maybe it's pride that's keeping you apart,' Annie pointed out. 'He may be sitting alone in his millhouse as full of regrets as you.'

'Who will?'

'Who?' Annie rolled her eyes.

There was a phone call for Merril a couple of days before the awards ceremony. It was her mother. 'Darling, I've just heard—why on earth didn't you tell me yourself?'

'I haven't won it. I'm simply a nominee,' Merril explained.

'But even so, it's wonderful. I'm so proud—may I come down?'

Merril went silent and her mother's voice came over the line again. 'Are you still there, darling?'

'Yes—but *what* did you say?'

'I wondered if I could be there on the night—it'll be quite like old tmes. But of course, if you're going to be with your friends . . . and—it doesn't matter . . .' Her mother's voice trailed to a whisper. 'I know we've had our disagreements in the past, and you'll be busy, I expect——'

'Mother? Listen to me. I'm just surprised, that's all. I thought you hated my job?'

'I don't hate it. I hate what it might do to you.'

She sounded as if she was about to hang up, but Merril nearly screeched into the receiver, 'Listen, of course you must come down! You still haven't seen my flat. And you must meet Annie. We'll do the sights together. And of course I want you to be here. Mother——?' There was a catch in her voice. 'I thought you hated what I'm doing and——'

'I know you did. You've simply never understood how frightened I am for you.'

'I'm so pleased you want to come up.' Merril gripped the phone as a sudden rush of emotion overtook her. 'But please, promise me one thing, you won't be disappointed if I don't win?'

After she had put down the phone she rocked back and forth on the hall seat with her knees drawn up under her chin, thinking about the harsh words that had passed between them over the years, the wall of misunderstanding built up brick by brick—and she began to see it in a different light. But it couldn't alter the fact that her mother had spent all those years at home, waiting for her father to come back, like the princess in the tower waiting to be rescued by a passing prince.

'Heavens, Merril, you look simply stunning!' Annie surveyed the effect from all angles before pronouncing herself satisfied. She had forced Merril to wear a simple white silk outfit with a wide-lapelled jacket that slipped off to reveal an almost backless short silk evening dress. 'You want something that'll take you from a formal dinner to a nightclub, and you don't want black, chic though it is. You want a colour to make you stand out in the crowd.'

'If I lose, I won't want to stand out——' said Merril.

'On the contrary. If you lose the main award, you may as well get the unofficial one for most stunning creature present. Now stop grumbling and put the jacket back on. It's time we had an aperitif before the horde arrive.'

The doorbell rang. 'That'll be Mother and her beau.' Merill flew to answer it. She had been surprised when her mother had rung back again to say that rather than stay at the flat with the two girls she would be booking into a nearby hotel with a friend. It had come out that the friend was male. Annie had put two and two together.

'If she's half as attractive as you, of course she'll have men-friends,' she mocked when Merril told her about the arrangements. 'She must only be in her early fifties—a very fashionable age these days.'

Now Merril found herself being introduced to a big, bluff stranger with a handshake that could crack the bones of an ox. But his face was sensitive and alive, and he was obviously mad about her mother.

'I'm afraid he's another newspaperman,' Millie Park confessed to her daughter as she sipped a gin and tonic while Ron made himself useful cracking ice-cubes in the kitchen. 'I do seem to be rather addicted to them, don't I? But this one is the stay-at-home kind, I'm pleased to say. I'm even doing a little writing myself these days,' she went on. 'Fiction actually, short stories.' Her eyes, the shade of blue Merril had inherited, began to sparkle. 'Ron's trying to get me to write a novel. I've always wanted to—but I never dared set pen to paper when your father was around. He was always so disparaging.'

'Father?' queried Merril.

Mrs Park gave her a long look. 'We ought to have a heart-to-heart one day. Your father wasn't the little tin god you seem to imagine.'

Ron came back then and soon it was time to leave.

Merril was so chock full of nerves, she scarcely noticed who Annie had picked out to escort her to the hotel where the ceremony was to be held. It was all one to her, she told herself fiercely. As soon as all this tomfoolery was over she would get back to her typewriter and get down to some serious work again. She would have to start scouring the papers for cheap flights as soon as her visa came through, and she couldn't wait to get on with it all.

Television cameras and a gaggle of press photographers were at the ready as they walked into the ballroom where the presentations were being held. The excitement of the occasion reminded Merril of a film première. She shivered, catching Damian's eye for a moment, noticing that he was escorting a rather pretty girl from Accounts this evening. Annie had somehow managed to get a table near the front, right next to the one reserved for the men who owned most of Fleet Street. 'I don't know how you do it,' said Merril.

'Charm, darling, nothing else.' Their table was quickly filled by the supporters she had rounded up. Mike was there, in a suit and tie, and he sportingly gave Merril a thumbs-up when she walked in.

'There's no beheading if you lose,' he told her, noticing her pale face, 'but you won't,' he added generously. 'I've got fifty quid on you.' He nodded towards Rory. 'And another fifty on him. I reckon *News and Views* are going to sweep the board.'

Merril scarcely recognised Rory without a bunch of cameras hanging round his neck. 'Don't you feel naked?' she asked, leaning across.

He pointed under his chair. 'Don't worry, I never go far without the life support system—and look here,' he turned, 'you haven't met the rest of it.' He introduced a small, dark-haired woman. 'My wife, Jeanie.' They shook hands. Jeanie was bright and pretty, not at all a faded princess waiting passively at home. Merril wondered what the secret was. But she didn't have time to ponder. With everyone sitting down it was a noisy, light-hearted crowd and she was soon swept up in a bantering dialogue with one of Cornel's stockbroking friends, who quickly got into swing of things, and for a little while Merril found herself almost forgetting that this was just a passing show from which she was longing to escape.

She reached out to look at the programme, but Annie put out a hand to stop her, then bit her lip. 'Go on, then. You may as well read it now. I've had the devil's own job to keep it away from you.'

Merril frowned. 'What's the mystery?' She quickly scanned the menu, and the order of toasts, feeling none the wiser, but when she reached the end she gave a little gasp, her blazing eyes turned full on Annie. 'You knew! You actually knew, didn't you?'

'I couldn't tell you. I'd never have got you out of the flat.'

'You're damned right!' Merril's hands were shaking. She read those last two lines again, just to make sure. 'Awards to be announced and presented by the actor Torrin Anthony.' That meant the lucky winner would have to shake hands with him, would have to withstand the lazy scrutiny of those honey-brown eyes . . . She was trembling so much, she had to hide her hands underneath the folds of the tablecloth. Everybody was laughing and talking, no one but Annie knowing of her turmoil. I won't win, don't let me win, she prayed.

The meal passed in a nightmare, scarcely registering. She rose for the toasts with everyone else, sat when they sat. Speeches were made. Television cameras lined up for the part of the evening everyone was waiting for. Merril couldn't see Torrin from where she was sitting, and she didn't try. Her head was bent most of the time and she felt as if she wanted nothing more than to crawl out of sight behind the nearest potted palm.

Then suddenly she heard his voice from the platform. It ran through her like an electric shock. Every hateful rise and fall scored into her brain with the pain of remembrance, his voice caressing her through those nights of love, nights she wanted to forget for ever. Nights of lust, she told herself, wondering miserably why everyone was suddenly turning to stare at her.

'Go on, you fool! Stand up and smile!' It was Annie, hissing at her across the table. 'You've done it! I knew you would!' Then she started to applaud like a wild thing, and it was taken up by the rest of the crowd.

Merril was aware of a sea of faces surging round her, and they were all smiling, everyone smiling, clapping, her mother's hand reaching out to squeeze her wrist, someone else leaning forward to kiss her, then her chair was being pulled back, and she found herself standing in a sea of light as a spotlight found her.

'Go to the platform, love.' It was Ron. She felt his hand propel her forward.

Then she was being carried on an ocean of applause to the foot of the platform where, if only she dared look up, she would see the man she most longed and most feared to see.

CHAPTER TEN

SHE was at the foot of the steps leading up on to the brightly lit platform before she dared raise her head. Then she saw a pair of black shoes, the unending length of his legs in the black trousers, a white cuff below the sleeve of a dinner-jacket, one hand clenched, then, suddenly, her head lifted and their eyes met, and it was as if the whole room had been plunged into silence. There was only the unending moment of his eyes meeting hers, the melting, the melding as his glance pierced her to the soul.

He seemed pale, she observed, striving for detachment. His hair was longer, blond and unruly. There were shadows under his eyes, hinting at depraved nights. But his smile dazzled over her as if there was no one else on earth he would rather be looking at. The old charm, Merril tried to criticise—switch it on, switch it off.

She counted the steps to the platform and moved towards his outstretched hand. The lips she knew so well were drawn back in a smile, and to her horror she felt him take her by both hands, pull her gently forward until their bodies were almost touching, then, taking his time, kiss her on both cheeks. Before she could recover, his hand strayed around her waist and he was turning her towards the sea of faces, encouraging their acknowledgement with a movement of his head.

There was no escape from the sensation of his hand on hers. Confused by the dazzle of flash bulbs, the television cameras moving in, the pressure of his hand never leaving hers, drawing her close, she could only count the seconds until such sweet agony should cease.

Torrin switched off the microphone round his neck, letting the applause continue, using it to make what he was telling her. 'I want to see you afterwards.'

'No chance. I'm with friends.'

'You must,' he insisted.

'No.'

'We'll see about that. You look ravishing, by the way. Have you been ravished recently?'

'How dare you? This is a public place!' Merril felt herself sneak a blushing glance at the people nearest to them. The applause was fading now, soon his voice, if he continued in this vein, would be booming out across the whole ballroom. She noticed him flick on his mike and hold up a hand.

In the ensuing silence he gave an outline of her short career, then she found a bronze trophy being pressed into her hands with another searing touch of those lips, and she was making a halting thank-you speech, words issuing from her lips like words of a foreign language, and then somehow the ordeal was over and she was stepping down off the platform, his hand steadying her, not leaving hers until the very last moment.

When she got back to her table she was trembling so violently that someone called for a triple brandy, then she was being kissed by all and sundry, passing off the chaotic tumbling of her emotions that made her shake so under the guise of excitement at winning the award.

Afterwards she was desperate to get away before Torrin could carry out his threat to talk to her, but there was an unending stream of well-wishers, hardened newspapermen shaking her by the hand, offers of jobs for which she would once have given

America's Favorite Author

Janet DAILEY

SWEET PROMISE

One kiss—a sweet promise
of a hunger long denied

83210 $3.25

SWEET PROMISE

*E*rica was starved for love. Daughter of a Texas millionaire who had time only for business, she'd thought up a desperate scheme to get her father's attention.

Unfortunately her plan backfired and she found herself seriously involved with Rafael de la Torres, a man she believed to be a worthless fortune hunter.

That had been a year ago; the affair had almost ruined her life. Now she was in love with a wonderful man. But she wasn't free to marry him. First of all she must find Rafael . . .!

her eye teeth. She supplied only the barest of answers as questions about her future plans were thrown at her, and then, with a sigh of relief, she saw Torrin being shepherded between the aisles, and at last the whole thing was coming to a close.

'What on earth was he saying to you when you went up there?' whispered Annie as they got up to go on to the nightclub as planned.

'Nothing,' Merril replied shortly.

'I've never seen you look like that before.'

'So?'

Annie gave a wicked smile. 'He certainly lives up to his reputation. I wouldn't mind joining his fan club myself!' She held Merril's arm, softening the effect of her words. 'You look fantastic. I set the video so you can see for yourself when we get back. I'll warn you, we're having a champagne breakfast!'

An orgy of celebration was the last thing Merril wanted. But there was obviously to be no escape. Dutifully she allowed herself to be swept along with the crowd. They had just reached the double doors at the exit when she felt someone push her from behind, and turning, she gave a gasp as she saw who it was bearing down on her.

'No, Torrin——' she protested as he took hold of her elbow beneath the full sleeve of her silk jacket and began to edge her out of the crowd. Ignoring her protests, he propelled her towards an empty alcove off the main ballroom.

It was littered with the debris of the celebrations—empty bottles, chairs askew, the air heavy with cigar smoke. A mirror behind his head threw back an image of her pale face turned to his.

'Well?' he growled.

'I've nothing to say to you, Torrin.'

He gave a leering smile as if he didn't believe her, and pushed her down on to one of the velvet-covered chairs against the wall, taking another one for himself and placing it directly in front of her so she couldn't get up without first pushing him out of the way. He straddled it, resting his arms on the back. 'So how does it feel to be flavour of the month?' he mocked, eyes licking over her angry face.

'Why ask me? You know only too well.'

'Merril——' He paused. 'I've missed you.'

'Obviously. That's why you've never been off the phone.'

'No,' he said slowly, 'I didn't ring you.' He didn't explain why not.

'I'm going on somewhere with friends now, so would you mind moving out of the way so I can join them?'

'Yes, damn you, I would mind!' For an instant his urbanity disappeared under a flash of anger, then the old charm reasserted itself. 'I'd like to see you again . . . please.'

Merril felt her throat contract. Looking at him now in his dinner-jacket, bow-tie undone, hair longer, thickening in rakish curls, she thought he looked like nothing so much as a small boy, crammed unwillingly into a wedding suit, eyes sparking with delightful devilment at the thought of mischief in the offing. He didn't mean to break hearts. He just couldn't help it.

'Say yes and stop teasing, angel——' he murmured, reaching out to take her hand in his.

'You honestly expect me to say *yes*?' she asked in astonishment. 'Why on earth should I? It was just part of the job, wasn't it? For both of us. Why have a repeat performance? You have hundreds of women throwing themselves at you the way I did. And as for me,' she shrugged, 'I was simply one that got lucky.'

'Merril—please!' There were thumb-prints of shadow beneath his eyes.

'Haven't you ever heard the word "no" before? Are you so used to flicking your fingers and having women fall at your feet, you can't believe it when someone actually turns you down?' She paused, humiliation at how completely she had given herself to him that weekend making her add words she would have erased at once if she could have. She said, 'I got the two things I wanted that weekend, Torrin. I got a view behind the scenes——'

'Yes, I read your article——'

'And,' she went on, ignoring his interruption, 'I got *you.*'

There was a pause.

'Merril . . .' His fingers slid over her wrist, fell.

'I've already told you I don't want to see you again. What would be the point?' she went on before he could continue. 'I don't hapen to regard myself as one of life's "little luxuries"—as you can see, I have a successful career of my own and don't need a man to make me feel important. I exist in my own right. Now move out of the way, will you?' she finished, as harshly as she could. 'This is becoming quite boring.' She was just about to try to push him aside when a voice interrupted.

'Tory, so this is where you're hiding! Come along, do! We're ready to go.'

Merril shot a bleak glance at the woman who stood in the archway. It was the one who had thrown herself all over Torrin after the first performance, the night they had met.

She was giving Merril a disparaging glance, and even Torrin must have been able to feel the air crackle with animosity. He rose slowly to his feet, silently offering a hand to Merril which she dashed to one side with an exclamation of disdain.

'Goodbye, Tory darling,' she said with as much sarcasm as she could muster as she stood up, 'it's been wonderful to see you again. Have a marvellous evening. Remember me to Tom——'

'It's not goodbye,' he said hoarsely, gripping her savagely by the arm, apparently oblivious to the hard stare his woman friend was giving him. 'I'll ring you.'

'You'll have to be quick,' Merril told him sweetly. 'I'm leaving as soon as I've fixed up a visa. I'm going back to Azur.'

Torrin looked stunned and his mouth opened, then closed. She took the opportunity to prise his fingers from off her arm, then, with a pitying look at the other woman, she swept out of the alcove to rejoin the celebrations.

'If it's anything you want to talk about—well, I am your mother.' It was mid-morning and Merril was still in bed, propped up on a pillow, riffling through the messages of congratulation that had come in with the post and trying to recover from the night before. The champagne breakfast had been a riot and she had managed to snatch only half an hour's sleep before the postman woke her. The trophy, draped in paper streamers, stood next to the bed. Banks of flowers made her bedroom look like a sickroom, she thought with a jaundiced glance round. She gave her mother a cheesy smile.

'I'm all right. It's just that, unlike you, I seem to have a penchant for falling for the wrong man.'

'Unlike me?' Her mother burst into a peal of laughter. 'My darling, that was my cardinal mistake. Look at me. Fifty-four—and what have I done with my life? I'll tell you,' she went on before Merril could interrupt, 'I frittered it away on a man who, wonderful though he was, would have preferred a professional servant to the amateur ministrations of a loving wife.' She looked contrite. 'Don't misunderstand—I wouldn't have chosen otherwise. But I can see now how your father sat on everything I wanted to do. He was such a dominant character. He would have been better off with someone more like himself, or no one at all.'

Merril didn't say anything.

'I can see I've shocked you. I did love him, Merril . . . Still do. No one will quite measure up, not even dear old Ron. But he was hell to live with—utter hell. I don't think I had a single night when I wasn't kept awake worrying about him, wondering if he'd come back to me dead or maimed—or whether he'd come back to me at all,' she added with a sideways glance. 'I used to blame his job, taking him off all over the world at a moment's notice. But it wasn't that. If he hadn't been a war correspondent he'd have been a racing driver or something equally foolhardy. I felt each day simply brought violent death closer. And I was right.' Her eyes glistened. 'As they tell us, if you can't stand the heat, get out of the kitchen. But I couldn't.'

'He always seemed wonderful to me,' said Merril in a small voice.

'He was—a marvellous man. And he adored you. But we were simply chalk and cheese. I'm the quiet, home-loving type. Sunday lunch at the golf club, that's my idea of excitement. He needed someone more robust, someone who could keep pace with him, with a similar taste for danger. That,' said Millie, taking Merril's hand in hers, 'is why I was so down on your journalism. I knew it would lead you into all kinds of adventures if you turned out to be anything like him. And I was right, wasn't I? I hoped to steer you into something less risky. But I should have known, you're a chip off the old block, darling. And although I know you're going to go on giving me sleepless nights, I know you wouldn't be happy living any other sort of life. Now,' she said briskly, 'what about this man whose name Annie breathed into my ear last night?'

'It's all over,' shrugged Merril.

'And whose decision was that?'

'Mutual, I suppose.'

'Annie tells me he was the one presenting the prizes?'

Merril nodded, wishing the conversation could be over.

'He certainly looked smitten when you went up——'

'Mother! He's an actor. It's his job to look smitten when there are women around.'

'Think carefully, sweetheart,' her mother warned. 'Ask yourself which is more important, pride . . . or love.'

This brief conversation gave Merril plenty to think about. Was her mother saying she should throw herself at Torrin and risk the harrowing pain of being discarded again? It was obvious from Torrin's attitude last night that he wanted a relationship of some sort. What sort didn't take much working out. It was as clear as daylight. His ego, deflated by her rejection, wouldn't let him rest until he had neatly ensnared her again. Then it would be the same thanks-and-goodbye performance as before.

The phone rang and Annie called from the sitting-room to say she would get it. A moment later she was holding it out to Merril with a meaningful expression. 'It's him!' she mouthed.

This time it was the voice Merril expected, sliding down the line with seductive sweetness, telling her how clever she was, how beautiful she had looked last night and finishing up with a suggestion for lunch that day, a celebration for winning the award.

'Look, Torrin, I don't think it would work. We both

want different things. And I've already told you I'm leaving as soon as I can. So what would be the point?'

'I thought you were waiting for a visa?' he asked.

'Yes, but——'

'Then see me once before you go. Please, Merril. See me now, this morning.' His voice seemed to shake. 'I must talk to you, darling.'

'I expect you're acting again. I must say it's very convincing.' Confusedly Merril realised she was on the point of giving in.

There was a pause and she expected to hear him repeat his invitation to lunch, but instead he said abruptly, 'You don't know what acting is. Forget it. I'm sorry I rang so early. I hope I didn't wake you.' The line went dead.

She sank back on to the pillow, her eyes sealed against the pain. Torrin could play her like a fish, offering the bait and, when he got her to the point of acceptance, snatching it away again, to leave her floundering.

The phone bleeped once more and she rummaged among the bedclothes for it with a sneaking hope that he had decided to give her another chance, but it was a foreign voice, and she had to strain to catch what was being said. Her heart leaped. It was someone from the Embassy. Her visa was ready and would she like to pick it up.

As she made arrangements to call in later that day she got an unexpected sinking feeling in the pit of her stomach. She hadn't worked her notice at *News and Views* yet, not having had the sense of purpose to inform Ray Doyle of her decision to resign. The response would be predictably fiery, and for a moment she saw the huge step she was about to take, opting out, they would say, at the start of a brilliant career. Then she thought of Torrin, the nightmare reality of knowing they were likely to keep on bumping into each other so long as she stayed in London. It would be no good living like that. It was best to make a clean break—to let the pain heal.

With an effort, she managed to force an image of Azur's rugged good looks into her mind, building up a picture of the way he had looked as they had said goodbye. The image was a little faded by time now, half real, half fantasy, distorted by imagination.

It'll have to do, she told herself . . . until the real thing comes along.

A few hours later she was sitting in a taxi bearing her along Baker Street, all the necessary proofs of identity in her bag. The visa would be waiting for her. It would take only minutes to pick it up. Then there was nothing to prevent her from getting out.

CHAPTER ELEVEN

THE TAXI was already crossing the park by the time Merril looked out to see where they were. It was a sunny day and London was making the most of it. Children tumbled and shouted on the grass, nannies in starched uniforms gossiped on benches beneath the trees, couples strolled arm in arm, people walked dogs. To Merril it spelled only heartbreak.

A red London bus cut in front of the cab and her driver drummed his fingers impatiently on the wheel before seeing an opening and thrusting them forward with a jolt that sent Merril rocking back. By the time she recovered he was turning off the main road into a tree-lined avenue, slowing as he drew level with the driveway of one of the white Georgian mansions just visible between the trees.

There was something familiar about the Embassy as the taxi turned into the drive. She rapped on the glass partition to attract the driver's attention. Slowly he brought the cab to a halt.

'This can't be the right address,' she told him as he pulled up and slid back the glass.

He reached out for the scrap of paper on which she had scribbled the address that morning.

'These embassies come and go,' he told her, handing the scrap of paper back. 'This is it, all right.' Silently he indicated a brass plaque on the wall facing them by the entrance. It was overhung with white blossom, but the name of the Embassy was clearly visible.

Merril slid back into her seat and let him take her

along the short oval drive to the foot of the steps. There was a uniformity about government buildings, and anyone could make mistakes, she told herself, but the neat circular flowerbed in the middle of the lawn seemed disconcertingly familiar.

An arrow and 'entrance' painted in bold black letters indicated which way she should go, and she went round the side of the building as directed, coming to an open door leading into a short corridor.

There was a bell push with a futher sign saying 'Ring for Attention', and one or two doors led off into other parts of the building. There was a perfume in the air like wax polish. A yellow duster lay on a windowsill where someone had dropped it. A bee bumped haphazardly against the window and there was a sense of flowers somewhere outside in the small courtyard on the other side. The air of tranquillity was unexpected after the rush and bustle of Fleet Street.

It would be quite possible, Merril told herself as she waited, for a portion of the building to be given over to flats. After all, a small country of little commercial or strategic importance would hardly be swamped with applicants wishing to visit it. The building was vast, probably far too large for their administrative requirements, but satisfying the instinct for prestige a foreign embassy required.

A door behind her was opened, interrupting these ruminations, and a woman in a long native caftan came in. Her appearance momentarily dispelled any doubts that Merril had come to the right place.

After stating her business she was at once conducted through one of the doors and along a corridor. She hoped they would have to cross the main entrance hall, for as soon as she set foot in it any lingering suspicions that it was the house where she and Torrin had had that first stormy interview would be dispelled.

But the woman showed her into a small waiting-room nowhere near the main entrance, ushering her in with a little bow of the head. She indicated that Merril would have a few minutes' wait and placed one or two travel brochures on a table beside her before she left.

Merril flicked through them. They were the usual sort of travel pictures, making a beautiful country look ordinary. Rory had put together a better selection for Jeanie while they were there. Even so, the sight of familiar places brought back a rush of memory.

Forgetting the pictures in the brochure, she closed her eyes, composing a series of snapshots of her own—Azur walking down a village street, a crowd of raven-haired children descending on him with screams of unmistakable delight—Azur hoisting two of them on to his shoulders and tucking another delighted brat upside-down under one arm as he kept on walking—Azur leading her to the top of the tower at dawn to watch the mist-wreathed valley come to life—Azur listening to the far-off sound of goat bells borne on the motionless air, turning to her as the sounds grew, as the sun touched the treetops in the valley. Then the sounds of the villagers themselves had begun to prick the silence—a herdsman's cry, a baby, the dry thud of someone chopping firewood—and all the time the white veil concealing the village was being peeled away by the hand of the wind, until at last the sun was full and red above the horizon and the whole village was revealed in picturesque detail.

He had kissed her then. It seemed a sacred kiss in honour of a world greater than themselves. They were dwarfed by the immensity of land and sky. It was at that moment Merril thought she loved him.

A sound in the corridor brought her back to the present. It was the same woman, indicating that Merril should follow her.

She led her to a door at the end of the passage and stepped to one side after she'd pushed it open. She left as soon as Merril went in.

Peering inside, she was unable to see much at first. The room was made shadowy by long curtains partly covering the windows and venetian blinds tilted against the sun.

There was an imposing desk in the middle of the room, a sense of gilding and cornices and heavy furnishings, and Merril wondered if she was to meet the ambassador himself. Her journalist's mind was already ticking over the questions she might ask him when a white-clad figure detached itself from beside the window, coming towards her, silhouetted against the blinds, but one hand unmistakably outstretched in greeting towards her.

The handclasp was brief though warm. Then she gave a gasp.

'We meet again.' The voice was husky, almost inaudible, and for a second it sent a shock of recognition racing through her. She put a hand to her cheek in confusion.

'It can't be——' she faltered.

'At your service.' The man gave an unexpected bow.

'Azur?' Hair prickled over her scalp. He was the last person she had expected to see. What on earth could he be doing in England?

'I understand you wish to go back,' he rasped.

'Yes . . . yes, I do,' she agreed, licking lips suddenly gone dry. 'As soon as possible.'

'No doubt it can be arranged.' He came closer. Seeing him garbed in the same attire as when she had first set eyes on him, with that guerilla-style scarf concealing his head and most of his face, she had an overwhelming feeling that she had landed in the midst of a dream. He put both hands to her shoulders and pulled her towards him. 'Merril . . .'

In the dim light she could see the eyes, bright with some sort of emotion, dwelling on her upturned face as he brought his arms around her. This had been something she had dreamed of so often in the last week or two as an antidote to Torrin Anthony that when it happened it seemed only a pale shadow of her imaginings. Paradoxically the dream seemed more substantial. She pulled back a little.

'Have you forgotten me?' he asked, voice vibrating with emotion.

Merril shook her head. 'No, never,' she admitted. It seemed to be the answer he required. Stifling her protests, her drew her firmly into his arms and held her close enough for her head to nestle against the soft stuff of the scarf covering his shoulders, and she could feel the beating of their two hearts in wild unison together. It was like coming home, yet, at that same instant, her mind was seared by a wild, compelling image of Torrin, and the way he had held her in just this fashion, stilling her anger, showing her a strength she had never forgotten. When she could, she drew back.

Azur let his hands slide reluctantly from around her waist. 'I've come for you. I'm taking you back with me . . . No protests, no objections,' he added masterfully, once again reaching for her.

It was so exactly what she had dreamed of, but now it was actually happening she felt herself hesitate. He saw her indecision and slowly let his hands fall to his sides.

In a turmoil of confusion Merril went over to stand beside the window, her back turned towards him. After an age she forced herself to speak. 'This is so difficult to say, Azur. You see . . . I met someone else when I returned home. You must think me imposs- ibly fickle—maybe it's true, but I really fell for him. Much against my inclinations. It's over now—but I know it's going to take some time for me to feel right about getting involved with anyone else. I don't think it would be fair to come back with you under these circumstances.'

'And this other man, my rival—his name?'

'Torrin Anthony.'

There was a pause, and Merril resisted the impulse to turn round. 'But if it's over between you?' he asked, his voice gruff.

'I can't come back—I thought I could. I thought it was what I wanted. But I see now it would be like running away . . . I have to stay to face up to the heartbreak, don't you see?' She turned slowly, then gave a gasp. 'Torrin!' she exclaimed on a different note.

'You never know when I'm acting, do you?' came the lazy response, in a voice that had lost all its adopted gruffness.

Pulling his disguise right down, he came rapidly across the room towards her. 'Thank you a million times for that, my darling. If the only way I can get you to say you care is to pretend to be someone else, then so be it.'

'Torrin, no!' Merril stepped back out of reach. The ground seemed to rock beneath her feet. She felt her fingers sliding down the wood panelling behind her.

Then his arm was coming out to support her and he was saying, 'No, don't give me that Victorian maiden act—it's so difficult to pull off without lapsing into melodrama.'

'I've never acted in my life,' she managed to whisper, 'and least of all now.'

He held her, not kissing her, just looking down into

her face.

She began to struggle out of his arms, her face a furious red. 'You must have been having a good laugh up your sleeve, you bastard!' she muttered hoarsely, spinning towards the door as she managed to loosen his grip. 'How could you play such a foul trick? I hate you! You're lower than a worm!' Tears of humiliation scalded her cheeks and she grappled with the door, trying to open it, but anger and humiliation making the simple task impossible.

He was beside her in two strides. 'Don't go——' He slammed the flat of his palm against the door, closing it. 'You can't think I did it to make you look a fool?' he said fiercely. 'Think back. When could I decently have told you we'd met——'

'Met? That's an understatement! Told me you were my "dream lover", you mean!' Her voice rose. 'Like when I came to interview you, for instance. You could have told me then. Like in bed—there was time enough, wasn't there?'

'Wait!' His face was like a thundercloud. 'How could I have told you at the interview? You didn't give me a chance before you launched into a diatribe against me.'

It was true. Merril remembered with anguished clarity the way she had cut him off in mid-sentence when he began by mentioning her piece about the civil war, and how she had gone on to treat him to a brand of sarcasm that was out of all proportion to the occasion.

'Your voice——' she said, looking bewildered. 'I would have thought I'd know that anywhere. It should have been a giveaway, despite your wildly different appearance, but you sounded so different——'

'Having a touch of laryngitis over in Kirkuk helped in that respect.'

Something came back to her. 'Of course, I remember Tommy saying something about a throat bug, but I put it down to the usual theatrical obsession with last-minute calamity.' Then she cast a glance round the room. 'This house—it is this one, isn't it? I thought it was, but I couldn't believe it . . .' She rubbed a hand weakly over her eyes. 'How come you were playing soliders?' she asked, trying to hide how unsure she felt.

'Maybe I'm playing actors?' he retorted ambiguously, then, more helpfully, 'I told you I was brought up over there. My old man was a diplomat, and until the age of ten I lived permanently out there. I went to the local school—made a lot of friends who've stayed with me all the way. Even when I was packed off to boarding-school in England I used to go back every holiday. Now, of course, a lot of those same friends are active in government, though not all of them on the same side. My sister happened to marry the man who is now Foreign Minister. When that little skirmish took place between two of the factions, it seemed idiotic not to try to mediate. You would do the same if you had two sets of friends who'd momentarily got themselves at cross-purposes. It's all over now. Those foreign troops you saw were sent ignominiously back over the border where they belonged. As for this place,' he looked round, 'my brother-in-law allows me to stay here whenever I'm in town.'

'And your name?'

'A childhood nickname.' He reached out and put a finger on her soft mouth. 'Couldn't you see how astonished I was when you walked into my dressing-room on the first night? I couldn't believe my eyes. I'd already decided that as soon as the show opened I was going to track you down. You seemed to cut me dead. It was only when I remembered I was still masquerading as Lord Rakewell that I understood why you didn't recognise me.'

'I thought you were simply switching on the charm——'

'Rakewell, arch-seducer? The first thing I said to you when we met here was how frightening it is to find people reacting so strongly to appearances but missing what lies underneath.'

'I didn't understand what you were trying to say.' Merril lifted her head, his finger sliding to the side of her neck, confusing her thoughts. 'If you remember, I tried to get my notebook to write it down——'

'I wanted you to respond to me, to forget your job, to see me as I am.'

'But you could have told me the truth later——' She tried to brush his hand away, not sure whether she ought to want it there.

'I tried to. I thought I'd set it up rather well, asking you to come here to do a profile. I thought it would be easier to explain if we met somewhere quiet—what better situation than an interview? But it misfired rather badly. That's when I had the crazy idea of kidnapping you. I thought the matter of my identity would come up naturally if we spent some time together.'

'But how could it? You looked so different. The first time we met you had long, scruffy hair and a blond stubble. Here you're clean-shaven with short hair or sporting a black stage wig with a pigtail. Have a heart, Torrin! Even your tan's faded.' She couldn't help giving a nervous smile at the sound of her own voice. It sounded as if she was forgiving him. But what would happen if she did? He was drawing her close again, her body taking fire from his.

She struggled, moving out of reach. 'I suppose you couldn't have told me when we spent the weekend together——'

'Things had changed by that time.' He frowned.

'Had they?'

For the first time he looked uncertain. 'I felt suddenly out of my depth. Of course I wanted you to want me. I knew I oved you. As I tried to tell you, for me it was love from that first moment when you threw yourself into my arms when the shooting broke out . . .'

'I threw myself? I thought you hauled me to safety?'

'Maybe it was mutual?' His voice was so quiet, it was almost inaudible. 'Later, after that argument at the millhouse when I saw that unmistakable look in your eyes, that hero-worship . . . it made me want to run. Can't you understand? I've had enough of all that. Everywhere I go women look at me as if I only have to raise a finger—and it's got nothing to do with me at all.'

'It doesn't seem a good idea to reject someone because they look at you with adoration in their eyes,' Merril said stiffly.

'I tried to explain—about not wanting responsibility, not wanting to have someone's happiness like a millstone round my neck.' He gripped her savagely by the chin and stared down into her eyes. 'Didn't you understand what I was saying?'

'You meant you wanted love without responsibility?' The words were muffled with a pain she couldn't conceal, but she had to understand what he was trying to tell her.

'I wanted our love to be equal—not a massive adoration on one side, half fantasy, half wishful thinking—something I could neither repay nor live up to. I wanted to be loved for *myself*, Merril. Not because I have a glamorous job, not for my looks, my physique, not for the parts I play—not for any of those reasons, because none of that has anything to do with the real me. Inside I'm just an ordinary fellow.'

'Clark Kent, not Superman?'

He smiled briefly. 'Yes, something like that.'

What he seemed to be trying to tell her was that he didn't want her to love him, that by loving him she put herself out of play. 'I can't help loving you,' she told him miserably. 'You *are* Superman to me. What's so wrong in that?'

'It's not true.' He turned to the door. 'Let's get out of this stifling room.' He led her out along the corridor and through a door at the back leading into a small courtyard. It was empty, but a fountain played, splashing muscially over smooth stones.

'Idyllic, isn't it?' he remarked ironically, sitting on the parapet and watching her closely.

'I suppose so.' Merril eyed the fountain and the fat yellow fish, noticing how the water boatmen were out already, leaping gaily over the surface of the water as if it were a skein of silk.

'What you're trying to say is, if I love you I lose you?' She trailed her fingers in the cold water, feeling that it matched her feelings, cold and flat. 'I believe I do love the real you,' she went on, no longer pretending. 'I must do, mustn't I, because half the time you're somebody else and I still go on feeling the same way. Our bodies know it . . . It's just our thoughts that keep us spinning away out of each other's reach.' She lifted her head. 'Maybe you simply like the idea of the hunt, Torrin. The idea of catching your prey doesn't interest you.'

'No,' he gripped her round the waist as if he had decided not to let her go, 'when I catch you I'm going to keep you.' She wondered how he could possibly think he hadn't caught her. But he held her for a moment before saying slowly, 'There is something else.'

He hesitated for such a long time, she wondered if she'd misheard, but, looking unseeingly across the courtyard to the house, he eventually said, 'I don't want to be a stand-in for your father.'

'*What?*' She slid off the parapet, looking down at him in astonishment.

'I think that's why a lot of marriages go wrong. One or both of the participants are looking for someone from the past. I don't want a six-month marriage, Merril. I have to slay that particular dragon . . . that's why I hoped for time before we became too deeply involved. I didn't mean to cut you out. It was to safeguard you as much as myself.' He was still fighting to express his feelings. 'I know how much he meant to you. He and Azur,' he grimaced, 'super-heroes, the pair of them. And distinctly uncomfortable bedfellows.'

'My father wasn't the little tin god I once thought.' Merril put a hand on his shoulder. 'I have it on the best authority.'

She had the satisfaction of seeing his head jerk up. 'What do you mean?'

'Mother had apparently the same idea as you about my feelings in that direction.' She had a far-away look. 'I suppose I did go on about him a lot. But it was all to do with my career. What he had achieved was like a guiding light when I didn't know how to set about things. His example showed me the limits I could go to.' She gave him a little smile and bent to rest her face against his cheek. 'I'm quite down-to-earth about most things, you know. It's only you who managed to send my common sense flying out of the window. As,' she mocked gently, 'you may have observed.'

Torrin took her hands, turning them over and kissing the palms. 'I want you unconditionally, Merril. Not because I fit some Identikit picture inside your head.' He said the words quietly, with force, and she met his eyes with loving recognition.

'You fit no picture. I think it was Tom who first drew my attention to that. You're an original.'

'Tom!' He laughed. 'He told me he saw you outside the theatre one evening, and he invited you backstage for a drink, but you refused.'

'I didn't dare come face to face with you. Not after you'd told me I'd thrown myself at you. I felt too ashamed. I really believed you meant it to be "kiss and goodbye".'

'I thought you wouldn't come because you really didn't care. He tried to make me see it wasn't so, but I couldn't believe him. It seemed obvious. Finally I couldn't bear it any longer. I decided to come round to the flat. But when I did you were out. It was a weekend, you must have been away. I sat outside all night in the car——' Torrin pulled her into her arms. 'I was in despair to know how to approach you. Then I was asked to present those awards and I thought that would be an opportunity to gauge how you really felt.' His eyes had a despairing look for a moment. 'Have you any idea of the agony I endured waiting to see you, sure you would reveal your true feelings when we met—only to find you were so violently against me? I felt I'd been right all along—you'd simply been infatuated with Torrin Anthony, actor, and like all such emotions, it had faded as rapidly as it had arisen. When we parted outside your office on the Monday morning you were so cool, accepting without a protest that it was just one of those brief affairs. I couldn't believe that was really you——'

'I wanted to plead with you to let me stay with you. But I forced myself to hold back, not daring to relinquish my last shred of pride. If you'd rejected me then, I would have been left with less than nothing,' she explained.

'And you say you never act? As a performance it was entirely convincing. And then later, at the ceremony, you really seemed to hate me——'

'By then I'd convinced *myself* I hated you. I believed you wanted me because I was now hard to get. You had to have everyone crawling in adoration at your feet, and you just couldn't take rejection.'

'My ego isn't that fragile. I can take rejection any time—it's part of the job.' He gave her a sudden look. 'At least, I can take it from anyone in the world—but not from you.' He held her in his arms, cradling her against him as if she were the most precious thing he possessed.

There was a call from across the courtyard, and a young woman with a baby on her hip appeared at a first-floor balcony.

'Torrin—you asked me to remind you when it was time.'

'My sister,' he told Merril. 'It's time to go to the theatre. Will you come with me?'

Later they drove slowly back to the millhouse, Torrin explaining that he didn't usually use the chauffeur-driven Jaguar so much, but that the injury to his ankle made it difficult to drive.

'And fly?' queried Merril.

'We'll test that out on Sunday,' he told her. 'I promised you flying lessons.'

'And other lessons?' she asked wickedly.

'Certainly other lessons. I always keep my word.'

'Torrin, what about the chauffeur?' she protested as he reached for her in the dark at the back of the car.

'He can take care of himself—if you'll take care of me.'

'I was rather hoping it would be the other way round, my——'

'That too, but first things first,' he broke in,

stopping her mouth before she could make any further protests.

It didn't seem to take any time at all to reach the millhouse. As far as Merril was concerned they could have driven all night. But once there she made a quick phone call to Annie to let her know where she was.

'I can tell from your voice everything has worked out.' Annie sounded pleased and went on, 'I've seen a wonderful hat in Harrods, just right for a wedding. And, Merril, I'm thinking of doing a feature on brides soon——'

'But Annie, he hasn't asked me yet!'

'Asked you what?' Torrin reached out and pulled her into his arms as she replaced the receiver on the bedside-table.

Merril shook her head and shivered as he began to undress her, taking his time about removing her clothes, peeling back each layer with a deliberate sensuality that brought her to the edge of suspense.

'No hurry,' he murmured, as she tried to lift her blouse to speed the moment when she would feel his mouth on her pulsing skin. He gripped both her hands in one of his and held them behind her back so that she was forced to let him take his time, unfastening one button at a time, planting kisses on each small revelation of naked skin, working his way with deliberate thoroughness towards her breasts, then teasing her nipples with his tongue until she gave soft moans of pleasure, curling against him to make him hurry.

'What haven't I asked you yet?' he murmured against her breasts, ignoring her pleas.

'Nothing.' Merril moved her head from side to side. 'Please, Torrin——'

'Merril, will you wear your pink dress again soon? I want to take it off you. You looked so delicious when you walked into my dressing-room. I don't know how I stopped myself from picking you up in my arms and running straight out of the theatre with you.'

'Yes, Torrin, anything, Torrin, but please——'

'Merril, could you tell I nearly punched that critic friend of yours when I saw him pawing you in the corridor? Then he had the effrontery to come up to me——'

'But you smiled at him!' Even now she could remember every detail of that electrifying smile.

'I had to. I could hardly start a brawl—I might have torn my silk jacket,' he added, lifting his head and giving her the smile. 'Just as I'm going to tear—this isn't your favourite slip, is it?'

'Torrin!' she gasped as the thin cotton was ripped the length of her body. Now she was wearing only the tiniest lace G-string. Torrin slipped a finger inside the elastic and she shivered as his fingers traced the delicate indentation it made over her hips.

'And when you came to interview me, why did you flare up when I kissed you? You kissed Azur like that. Even though you denied it!'

'It's because I remembered him that I—that you—he—I mean—— Oh, hell, Torrin, I can't think when you do that!'

'I thought it was a good sign when you said my name twice in a non-sarcastic manner,' he murmured huskily against her throat while his hands went on doing unimaginable things to her. 'I feared you were going to call me Mr Anthony for evermore. Did you know the second time you called me Torrin you said it with a certain inflection . . . it told me such a lot about the way you were beginning to feel about me—at least, I told myself it did.'

'That must have been just before you frightened me so much that I fell into the millrace,' she murmured, sighing, as the lace nothing of the G-string slid down her thighs. 'But when you dragged me out you were horrible to me——' She twisted to look at him, his lips now trailing sweet fire along the path made by the scrap of lace as it slid over her ankles. 'And just when I'd begun to accept that I didn't care a damn any more about Azur, or anyone but you——'

She moved against him, unable to help herself.

'No, don't rush. Slowly, like this.' He was still tracing the imaginary pattern her lace panties had made, but in a different way that sent all thoughts out of her head.

'Torrin, please——'

'Slowly, my love . . . You were so definite about despising me, I thought it was permanent. Then when you changed I thought it was the old hero-worship coming to the surface. I couldn't bear the thought that you loved the image, not me at all.'

'And then at the hotel you tried to warn me off, didn't you?' she whispered, trying to slow her movements to match his own.

'But you ignored me, you wilful child—until next morning, when you realised what you'd done.

'I felt terrible. I could guess what you were thinking—just another notch on the bedhead——'

'That is so insulting—did you expect me to be so shallow?'

'I was too miserable to think straight——'

'I have to confess I did take advantage of your lustful ways,' he told her. 'I was ashamed afterwards. I knew I could have rushed you into anything, but I was sure it wouldn't have lasted.'

'I thought you'd changed your mind. Torrin, do that some more. It's heavenly!'

'I dared not pressure you, but I was longing to kidnap you all over again. I thought we managed the goodbye with a certain style—except that I'd had no intention of saying goodbye. It was like suddenly finding yourself in the last act of a different play.'

'Why didn't you ring me?' she asked.

'At first I told myself it was for the best. It was what you seemed to want. Then the truth began to dawn—*I* needed *you*—but I no longer knew what you felt. Had it been just one of those casual flings? Or did you really care?'

'If you'd known what I was going through—I couldn't believe it when I saw your name on the awards programme,' Merril told him.

'Don't mention that night! It was the blackest of my life. I really thought everything was lost. You were totally convincing when you told me you'd been notching up a score—with me! You were like an ice maiden. For a moment I felt demented. Then you dropped that bombshell about going back to Azur . . . I didn't know what the hell to make of that. But it was the same old thing—I wanted you to respond to *me*, not to some super-hero—even if the super-hero was me! But by then I was thinking, if the only way I can have you is to let you believe I'm something I'm not, then, what the hell, I'll go with it. I had to have you. For keeps.'

In the rose light from the lamp she saw him frown a little. 'And that was the problem. I still couldn't convince myself your feelings would last—not even for Azur . . . but again I thought—better a six-month marriage with her than nothing at all. I was willing to do anything, *be* anything you wanted. I would have played King Kong if it had meant you'd love me.'

'That would be interesting,' said Merril, twisting on top of him so he could take each breast lovingly to his mouth. 'And I can see now why you were so cynical about my feelings—all that fan mail!—but even that should have convinced you that feelings do last. You're a dream lover to so many women, Torrin, because they guess what you're really like under the mask. Nothing can disguise that.'

She gave a gasp as he slid her underneath him, both hands pressing into the pillows on either side of her head.

By now Merril didn't want to talk any more. She simply wanted to fly, wherever Torrin chose to pilot her into the upper reaches of the seventh heaven.

But he lifted his head one last time. 'Now will you tell me what it is I haven't asked you yet?'

'It's all right, I think you already have——' she breathed.

'And will you? Marry me, I mean?' he asked tenderly.

'Torrin, what are you doing?'

His voice was husky. 'I'm giving you a lesson in love.'

'Let it last for ever, my dream lover,' she whispered, moving sensually beneath his touch. 'Like our marriage.'

'And like my love for you,' he murmured in velvet tones beside her head.

And as she moved against him, all notion of holding back now gone, she knew that, like love, their dream would last for ever—because it was the real thing.

Harlequin Presents.

Coming Next Month

Available in October wherever paperback books are sold, or through Harlequin Reader Service:

In the U.S.
901 Fuhrmann Blvd.
P.O. Box 1397
Buffalo, N.Y. 14240-1397

In Canada
P.O. Box 603
Fort Erie, Ontario
L2A 5X3

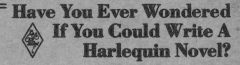

Have You Ever Wondered If You Could Write A Harlequin Novel?

Here's great news—Harlequin is offering a series of cassette tapes to help you do just that. Written by Harlequin editors, these tapes give practical advice on how to make your characters—and your story—come alive. There's a tape for each contemporary romance series Harlequin publishes.

Mail order only

All sales final

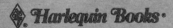